'Nervous?'

'Certainly not,' An

'Liar. You're shaking.' Dr Duncan Hunter took hold of her hand and, to her utter humiliation, her fingers were trembling. His thumb was on her pulse point, aware that her heart was racing. It was only the lightest of touches, casual and without meaning. Yet she was acutely aware of the man, big and bulky in his survival suit, and longed, for one wild instant, to be closer.

Dear Reader

Nature gets its own back this month! Stella Whitelaw's DELUGE takes us to the dangerous waters of the North Sea, and Meredith Webber's WHISPER IN THE HEART includes a terrifying bush fire! There's water in HEARTS AT SEA by Clare Lavenham, following a cruise ship, but STILL WATERS — despite the title! — by Kathleen Farrell brings us to earth in Edinburgh. All good stuff for you to enjoy.

The Editor

!!!STOP PRESS!!! If you enjoy reading these medical books, have you ever thought of writing one? We are always looking for new writers for LOVE ON CALL, and want to hear from you. Send for the guidelines, with SAE, and start writing!

Stella Whitelaw's writing career began as a cub reporter on a local newspaper. She became one of the first and youngest women chief reporters in London. While bringing up her small children, she had many short stories published in magazines. She is deeply interested in alternative medicines, and is glad that her son, now a doctor and anaesthetist, has an open mind about them. A painful slipped disc has improved since practising the Alexander Technique daily.

Recent titles by the same author:

A CERTAIN HUNGER
DRAGON LADY
THIS SAVAGE SKY

DELUGE

BY

STELLA WHITELAW

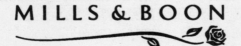

MILLS & BOON

MILLS & BOON LIMITED
ETON HOUSE, 18–24 PARADISE ROAD
RICHMOND, SURREY, TW9 1SR

MILLS & BOON, the Rose Device and LOVE ON CALL are trademarks of the publisher.

*First published in Great Britain 1994
by Mills & Boon Limited*

© Stella Whitelaw 1994

*Australian copyright 1994   Philippine copyright 1994
This edition 1994*

ISBN 0 263 78760 5

*Set in 11 on 13 pt Linotron Times
03-9409-43630*

*Typeset in Great Britain by Centracet, Cambridge
Made and printed in Great Britain*

CHAPTER ONE

'GET behind that screen and take your clothes off, please. Down to the waist will do. And be quick. I've got a lot of people waiting.'

Andrea West drew in her breath sharply. She was certainly not going to take her clothes off. She saw a broad figure hunched over a file, writing furiously, a thatch of dark hair fallen across eyes that were masked by glowering eyebrows. He was dressed, unprofessionally for a doctor, in a crew-necked jersey and an ancient tweed jacket.

'Hurry up, please. I haven't got all day. There's a whole new intake of crew to see.'

Andrea perched hesistantly on the edge of a chair like a bird, knowing she might doze off if she leaned back. The last twenty-four hours had been a rush of packing, travelling, the flight north and she had had precious little sleep. She watched his long brown fingers moulding the pen backwards and forwards as he collected his thoughts before charging into another paragraph of scrawled notes. He had the usual dreadful, unreadable handwriting.

It gave her a chance to study Dr Duncan Hunter. All she could see was weatherbeaten skin, a strong, straight nose and jutting chin, and thick dark hair streaked with silver over his ears. A chin like a cliff—angular, stubborn and awkward. She was glad she would not be working with him.

'I don't know why women want to work on rigs,' he muttered, pulling her file towards him. 'It's noisy and dangerous. Why don't you cook on shore? There are plenty of hotels and restaurants crying out for decent cooks.'

'I am not a cook,' Andrea said. She stifled a yawn as waves of tiredness caught up with her in the small and stuffy surgery. Dawn had been washing a faint colour over the rooftops as the plane had landed at Aberdeen. The other passengers had been mostly men, roustabouts who worked on the rigs. They had heaved themselves up, stretching and groaning and rubbing the grit out of their eyes.

'You have to keep moving, miss,' the bearded youth who had been sitting next to her had said. 'Give your legs a good rub, get the circulation going. There's plenty of work in Aberdeen. Get a steady job and you'll be sitting pretty.'

His cheerful words had made Andrea's spirits soar. She was already sitting pretty. She had an interesting, responsible and extremely well-paid job ahead of her.

A loud cough broke into her thoughts. 'If you are unable to keep awake for your medical now, I suggest you kip down somewhere else,' Dr Hunter said, barely keeping the exasperation out of his voice. 'There's a couch outside. Of course, you may lose a day's pay.'

Andrea jolted herself upright, bringing her thoughts to the present. She willed her voice into an even calmness.

'If you look at my file properly you will see that I am not here to work as a cook,' she said evenly. 'This medical is wasting your time as I have all my recent medical records with me.'

'Cleaner, steward, whatever. Though they are mostly married women with grown-up families who want to get away from domestic life. You don't look old enough to have a family, not even a small one.' He glanced briefly at the file in front of him. 'Roll up your sleeve, please, Miss West.'

He unwound the sphygmomanometer and slapped the cuff-wrap round her arm before pumping in air to create pressure, locating the brachial artery on the inner side of her biceps muscle with a stethoscope. She felt transparent, invisible.

'Most doctors pay attention to what is being told to them,' said Andrea, watching the gauge with professional interest. 'All my notes are here. I had a full medical before I left St Jude's last month.'

'Quiet, please. I'm listening for the systolic level.' He pumped in more air with a gesture of annoyance. Andrea waited for the pressure to drop off.

'St Jude's sent my medical records ahead,' she repeated slowly and distinctly. 'None of this is necessary.'

'St Jude's?' he said, charting the result.

'St Jude's Hospital. I'm sure you've heard of it; it's one of London's most famous teaching hospitals. If you had read my file properly, you'd have realised that I'm the new medic for the Lochinvar rig.'

His glance shot up. A look of astonishment crossed Dr Hunter's face followed fast by another of utter disbelief. His eyes went as black as sea pools, dark brows bristling. A North Sea thundercloud gathered on his face, stitching up the frown lines.

'But we don't employ women as medics on the rigs. It's quite out of the question. Unfortunately I was away all last week. I'd better check. Don't bother to undress. You may be on the next plane home.'

'I don't think so. I have a contract with Columbus Petroleum Corporation. Since I sent a photograph with my CV, the appointment of a woman can't have been a mistake. And it's not that unusual for a woman to work on a rig. In Norway, most of the medics are women.'

'This isn't Norway,' he snapped, shutting her

file. 'This is Aberdeen and the inhospitable North Sea and we don't risk women on the rigs.'

'Excuse me, Doctor, I think you mean that you don't like them. I believe you'll find that statistics now show that women have a beneficial effect on a rig. Safety factors improve and it's a well-known fact that a female presence improves the working and leisure atmosphere.'

'This appointment has been made over my head and without consultation,' he said, tapping his pen impatiently on the desk, shuffling notes. 'I'll have to look into it.'

'I was told that the situation was urgent, that Lochinvar rig is without a permanent medic. That's why I rushed up here, to replace the temporary medic.'

For the first time Dr Hunter looked at her properly. She stared back at him, putting on her formidable Sister-in-Charge expression. She knew she had a strong face with dark, well-defined brows. Many a junior nurse had discovered exactly what Sister West meant by the rising angle of her brows.

What Andrea did not realise was that her grey eyes were deeply beautiful and her full mouth vulnerable and gentle in repose. It was a face full of contradictions. Dr Hunter saw them all and was thrown. For a moment he was astonished by the feelings that surged through him.

'You're much too young,' he said abruptly, his

size ten feet now firmly back on familiar ground. 'And much too thin and bony. You wouldn't last five minutes on a rig. It's a tough job. I shall have to look into the appointment. Perhaps we can find you a shore post.'

Andrea nearly exploded. 'For heaven's sake, Dr Hunter, women are quite capable of taking on the most challenging of jobs. Do you think we still wear bonnets and shawls and spend Mondays at the wash-tub with a scrubbing-board? Aberdeen isn't the back of beyond. Some of the good news must have filtered through.'

'Are you challenging my authority?'

'Yes, Dr Hunter. I want this job. I've been a sister on Accident and Emergency for nearly three years. I've worked in Eye and Ear Units which will have particular relevance for rig work. As for being much too fragile, that's laughable. I'm five feet eight with muscles to match.'

Andrea knew that that was an exaggeration. She was slim but strong. A nurse needed to be strong in A & E. There were never enough orderlies or porters for all the lifting and shifting. A sister had to be prepared to do anything in an emergency. A rush of casualties from an accident could strain their resources.

'Medics on rigs have a huge responsibility,' Dr Hunter went on as if he had not listened to a word. 'There's a sizeable male workforce and anciliary staff. I don't need someone with simple first-aid who will call me out every five minutes for permission to put on a plaster.'

Andrea swallowed her indignation. 'I'm capable of normal medical procedures entirely on my own, including suturing and intravenous. If you are the land consultant for the rigs, then I shall restrict my calls for only the most serious emergencies. You are obviously far too busy.' She made her voice heavy with sarcasm but her eyes were lit with determination. 'My calls will be as few as possible.'

'Onshore consultant,' he corrected.

Andrea rolled down her sleeve and fastened the neat cuff. 'So, do I get to go to Lochinvar? I'd like to fly out today. I've wasted enough time already.'

A sudden gleam of amusement in his dark brown eyes took Andrea by surprise. Surely the man didn't have a sense of humour? But the moment passed and Andrea wondered if she had imagined it. 'Your persistence is intriguing. I'm curious.'

'I simply want the job and it's mine. I've been officially appointed,' Andrea said, her eyes blazing.

'And you can be officially unappointed just as fast. I'm one of those consultants who make regular calls on all the rigs. And until you leave, I'll definitely be taking the helicopter shuttle out to Lochinvar on a daily basis. I'm not leaving you on your own to cope with an eighty-strong drilling workforce and the anciliary support staff.'

'I'm perfectly capable,' said Andrea, but her heart fell, beating irregularly. Not every day? She couldn't stand the thought of seeing this arrogant man every day. Settling into a new job was hard enough without his interference. As it was, she knew she had a lot to learn, and she did not want him watching her every move. The alien environment was in itself a challenge. And the noise. . . she had to learn how to cope with the constant noise.

She might even get seasick some of the time. . . until she got used to the swell of the sea. And she was still in the throes of learning to live with her unsettled heart after the hurt caused by Lucas Dereham. The pain rarely left her. Now there was this insufferable Dr Hunter to contend with as well. Life was not fair. Then she thought of the money and the row of lovely noughts on her pay-cheque. She knew it was mercenary but that was what she had had to become.

'Stay there while I check with someone,' he said. He got up. He was as tall as she had thought. 'I suppose you're just doing it for the money,' the doctor said, reading her thoughts.

'Aren't we all?' She was equally abrupt.

'Putting in for a time-share apartment in Spain?'

'No, a Victorian grade two villa in Hastings.'

He was nonplussed by her reply but Andrea did

not feel inclined to explain. He went out of the surgery and it seemed that he was gone a long time. His face was set into disapproval when he returned. He took her medical report and glanced through it.

'It seems it's an emergency appointment. . . only for the time being. Well, I suppose I can accept this. You'd better get out to the helicopter port. Ask outside for your papers, kit etc. Hard-hat and ear-protectors on for all outside work, Miss West, or you'll be stone-deaf in weeks.'

'Sister West,' said Andrea, rising quickly, finding her tiredness had quite gone. The ascerbic doctor had reactivated her adrenalin and the contract was for a year. She did not correct him.

She took one last look before she left, hoping that there was some semblance of a human being in the big man. But he was head down again, writing at speed. He had already forgotten her. She was no more than an irritation, like a mosquito that buzzed around in the night.

Andrea went outside the doctor's surgery, back into the hubbub of ColPet's personnel office. She had to collect her kit, find the helicopter port and by this evening she ought to be aboard the Lochinvar. Suddenly she was nervous.

It had all happened so quickly. A telegram had arrived from ColPet inviting Andrea to telephone and reverse the charges. They were desperate for a medic on Lochinvar. The medical officer had

had to rush home due to a family emergency and no rig could function without a medic on board.

'Don't even stop to pack,' the personnel officer had said on the phone, obviously pleased to have found such a well-qualified replacement. 'All your kit will be here for you to collect. Fly up immediately. Get a standby ticket.'

'Are you sure you're doing the right thing?' her mother, Florence West, had asked anxiously. 'Aberdeen's such a long way away and those rigs look so dangerous. Couldn't you get a local job?'

'Medics are there to promote safety,' Andrea had said, mentally packing. 'It's one of their most important roles, not just clearing debris out of someone's eye or putting a spot of ointment on dermatitis. My job will be to prevent those injuries in the first place.'

And a long way away was just where Andrea wanted to be. As far away from the righteous and upright Lucas Dereham as possible. It hadn't helped her to get over him, seeing him cruising around the hospital every day. It had been a wrench leaving St Jude's but he had made it quite impossible for her to stay on.

'Take plenty of warm things,' Mrs West had said, hovering in the doorway of her daughter's bedroom. 'It'll be really cold in Aberdeen.'

'Not all the time,' Andrea had replied, throwing a pile of shirts and hand-knitted sweaters into a big zipper bag. 'Aberdeen has a lovely climate;

it's a city full of flowers and parks and river walks, and you can't grow flowers without sun and warmth.'

'I don't like you going all that way. . .'

'It's only for a year, Mum, and think of all that money I'm going to earn. Think of what we are going to do with it. We need that money. It's a lifeline for both of us and you know we need it.'

Working on an oil rig was the quickest way for a nurse to earn a substantial sum of money, Andrea reminded herself as she queued for her kit at ColPet. But she was nonplussed to find that there was no regular medical uniform as she was issued with yellow overalls, boots, hard hat etc.

'No uniform?' she asked, thrown.

'It's all very casual on board. Starch is out. Medics wear what they like in surgery and sick-bay. Times have changed, Sister West.'

'So it would seem.'

But not for me, thought Andrea, remembering the two pristine white coats she had pushed into her bag as an afterthought. They would be her uniform worn over jeans and a shirt. A starched apron and wings might be out of place on an oil rig but her training was that medical personnel gained authority in uniform. She had a feeling that she was going to need that extra professional look to boost her confidence. Eighty men. . .and she would be responsible for their health.

She was going to be in full charge of both

surgery and sick-bay. The responsibility of what she had taken on was awesome. Eighty oil rig workers and twenty support staff, many of whom were women. But there was always Dr Hunter or one of the other consultants to contact by radio if she was in trouble, and she would make very certain that such an occasion did not arise if she could help it.

Andrea smiled to herself, the first smile for weeks. She was going to make doubly sure that she could cope without the awkward Scots doctor in attendance.

She took the crew bus out to the heliport. There were buses to and from the airport all day. She reported immediately to the check-in desk and found the ColPet representative. He was helpful with advice and tips.

'Take a selection of today's newpapers on to the rig with you,' he said. 'Everyone is starved of news to read, even with television on most rigs.'

'What's the weather like today, out there?' Andrea asked. It had already turned chilly and she zipped up the collar of her padded scarlet anorak.

'Don't worry. Not too rough. If the flight has to be cancelled then you'll be accommodated in a decent hotel for the night. One more civilised night.'

Her appearance at the heliport was causing interest and Andrea hoped desperately that the

wait would not be too long. She was not used to
so many pairs of male eyes staring curiously in her
direction and evaluating her female charms. A
coldness crept into her grey eyes, a steely stiffness
invading her spine and she resisted all advances
with a cool but polite, 'Hello.'

She knew that she was in for a tricky year on
the rig. And the first two weeks would set her
style and reputation. She had to maintain a professional distance, but at the same time be friendly
and approachable.

The Customs search came as a surprise.

'Why?' Andrea asked. 'An oil rig perched in
the middle of the North Sea is not exactly going
abroad.'

'It's so you don't take anything on board which
will be a danger to you or the rest of the people
on the rig,' explained a member of the security
staff. 'No alcohol, no drugs, firearms, explosives.
That sort of thing. You'd be surprised what people
try to smuggle aboard.'

'I guess that makes sense.'

Andrea was then instructed how to put on the
bulky orange survival suit and how to wear a life-
jacket. She listened intently, aware that if the
chopper ditched, her life would depend on following the safety procedure and knowing what to do
in an emergency.

By the time she had taken in the helicopter

landing officer's instructions for boarding the helicopter, her head was spinning with information.

'Remain in view of the pilot when approaching the bird and follow the correct route to the entrance door,' he said finally. 'Good luck, Sister. They need you out there. A rig is like a big city. Only don't try looking for any underground trains. You could get wet.'

Andrea tried on another smile. The voices of the other flight passengers braided together and she kept close to the group. For the first time the actual danger involved really came home to Andrea. Travelling out to a rig was fraught with complications and she was nervous enough about her first flight in a helicopter. No one else seemed bothered. The men were talking and joking in clusters, as if the whole thing was a joy-ride and the noise was charged with an almost pre-holiday excitement.

'Nervous?'

'Certainly not,' she said without turning.

'Liar. You're shaking.' Dr Duncan Hunter took hold of her hand and to her utter humiliation, her fingers were trembling. His thumb was on her pulse point, aware that her heart was racing. But the feeling was not simply fear of the flight ahead; it was a new and totally unexpected treachery that came from within her. She could not think clearly. It was only the lightest of touches, casual and without meaning. Yet she was acutely aware of the man, big and bulky in his survival suit, and she longed, for one wild instant, to be closer.

Survival suit? Surely he wasn't flying out with them? Not checking up on her already?

He turned her hand over as if gauging the ability of her slender fingers.

'I'm simply cold,' she said defiantly, snatching her hand back. 'I'm not used to this weather. I've come from the south. It's much warmer there.'

'Put your gloves on. Don't get cold, especially your feet and hands.'

Hastings seemed a million miles away. The tall wooden fishermen's net sheds on the shore, the old houses—Georgian, Edwardian and Victorian—cluttering the raised pavement of the high street. Suddenly Andrea felt homesick for the place where she had grown up as a child.

'I thought I'd see how you were getting on,' said Dr Hunter.

'I'm a big girl now. I can travel by myself.'

His eyes glanced over her as if to confirm her size. She coloured, knowing that the bulky survival suit made her look three times as large. It was not fair. Dr Hunter's six feet plus simply made him look more confident and capable in the suit, his powerful shoulders moving with easy strength. Now that she was standing beside him, she became more aware of his rugged good looks. He was a true Scot, his colouring, his height, his soft brogue, his fierce independence and unnerving determination to have things his own way.

'You could still change your mind,' he said. 'It's not too late. They'd understand. It's no place for a woman. You wouldn't be the first to get cold feet. Men are the same. Persistent pains which defy diagnosis sometimes miraculously clear up the moment they get ashore.'

'How kind of you to be so understanding and sympathetic,' said Andrea drily, trying to smooth the bulky garment down over her narrow hips. 'But I'm not changing my mind and it's no use trying to get rid of me. I'm here for a year, then I might return to civilisation and the politeness of London consultants.'

He gave her an abrupt, dismissive glance, as if her remark was not worth answering.

'Your year will be the shortest on record. Sister West will be radioing to be taken off long before her first hitch is over. Fourteen days is a long time if you are repeatedly hung over the side with seasickness. Even good sailors are affected by the rough weather.'

'What a charming way you have of putting things. How your patients must love your sensitivity. An oil rig isn't a ship or a boat. It's not moving. It's not going anywhere.'

'Didn't you know that Lochinvar is a semi-submersible?'

The doctor looked amused again and Andrea

heard an overwhelming clang of doom in her ears. Her heart gave a downward lurch. He gave her a sidelong glance.

'A semi what?'

'A floater. Its hulls are submerged in the water and not resting on the sea-bed, more like a huge floating ship. There is periodic weather swaying. They're used out here because of their stability for drilling in these wild and hostile waters. Of course, they are anchored to the sea-bed after they are positioned exactly over the well head.'

'Thank you for making me feel immeasurably better,' said Andrea, her throat dry, her candid grey eyes matching his coolness. 'You certainly have a gift for putting people at their ease. I hope you have the same success rate with your patients.'

'I haven't lost any yet due to my inborn honesty,' he said mildly. 'And, as you so rightly say, it is a gift.'

'And I'll be equally honest,' said Andrea. 'I'd be obliged if you would just leave me alone to get on with my work. I don't need your help and I certainly don't need you breathing down my neck at every opportunity, waiting for me to do something wrong.'

At that moment, the boarding announcement crackled over the tannoy. The Sikorsky S61N was ready to take off. Andrea, carrying her zipper bag, turned away to join the cluster of people travelling off shore. The bag contained all she would need for the next fourteen days. . .her first hitch. None of the men offered to carry her bag and she was glad. She was their equal. She could carry her own bag.

The dos and don'ts of boarding echoed in her head and she repeated them to herself: remain in view of the pilot when approaching the helicopter; don't pull or slam the door; don't approach the tail-rotor area; don't touch any levers.

The big red white and blue machine was bigger than she had expected, the rotor blades moving idly. Her bag was stowed away in the luggage hold and she climbed aboard the cramped cabin. It was nothing like a commercial airline. She made sure that the lifejacket was firmly fastened round her waist. She had so much on, she could hardly breathe. Then there were earplugs to put in and earmuffs to wear. This was turning into an ordeal of mammoth proportions.

Dr Hunter was sitting the other side of the aisle. He tugged at her sleeve and pointed to her seatbelt. He mimed that it should be fastened underneath her life-jacket. She struggled to get it right. Duncan leaned over and deftly fastened the clasp. She felt his breath fan her cheek and drew back swiftly.

The steward was still closing the doors as the engines began to rotate the blades. He did not seem to be in the least concerned as the helicopter began to rise before the doors were fully closed, the earth below tilted clearly in sight. He hung like an acrobat for a second before swinging himself inside.

The whirlybird backed off with a strange reverse pull sensation before wheeling sideways and taking off towards the sea. After her first apprehension, Andrea found she was enjoying it. The views of the granite coastline were magnificent. Then they were flying over the silvery sea, arrows of light piercing the clouds.

Her mind went into neutral. It was three months since her father had died. As she flew over the pulsing sea, those last peaceful days came back to her more strongly than ever. Her career had taken her away from home but those last days had been a rebonding, a chance to get to know each other again, and although they both knew that he was dying, neither had realised that time was so short.

'I'm so sorry I haven't been able to get home more often,' Andrea had told him. The last year had been a madness of yearning for Lucas. Always hanging around in case she could see him, in case there was a chance of a few hours together.

'You don't know how much your mother and I have missed you.' Her father had looked so pale and wan against the hospital pillows, yet his smile had been just like hers, and his eyes. Andrea had the same grey eyes. They had smiled at each other and she'd taken his hand, holding the frail, bone-white fingers carefully.

'How much I've always loved my little girl,' he'd said. 'Your lovely hair and your pretty ways. And I was so proud of you when you went away to train as a nurse. I knew your work was important and every. . .step of your career was. . . source of pride. . .'

He'd stopped, gasping for breath, and Andrea had gently put the oxygen mask over his mouth till his breathing had settled again. He pushed it away.

'There isn't much time, Andrea. I have to tell you. There's something I must tell you. . .'

'Not now, Dad. You ought to rest. I'll be here. I won't leave you. . .'

He'd smiled at her and she'd curled her other hand over his fingers so that her warmth would reach his heart. At some time during the evening, her mother had joined her and they'd sat together, quietly, knowing that his life was ebbing away.

Some time during the night, Andrea had dozed off. When she'd awoken, stiff and aching, her father had gone. Her dreams and her childhood had gone with him.

She wept for the time she had wasted, and the love she had never appreciated. She had wanted to say more than goodbye. For a while she'd cradled him in her arms, hoping his spirit still hovered around. There were many stories on the wards that gave her hope that her love could still reach him.

Dr Duncan Hunter watched the tears slipping down Sister West's cheeks and was appalled at what he had done. He stared out of the cabin window, wondering why he had become so hard-hearted. He was against women on the rigs, especially medics. The intimate nature of the work was not a woman's job and they could cause trouble among the men. He wanted Andrea West to go away but he had not meant to make her cry.

Andrea turned away to look out of the cabin window, blinking back her tears. In the distance was a huge and daunting shape, rising from the sea on sturdy legs. It rose from the sea to a great height, a frontier of technology, a city at sea.

Suddenly all its lights came on and it was a fairyland of decks and platforms, catwalks, stairs and pipes and ladders, the swirling seas lapping round its feet like a molten gold lava, a mist of glistening spray shrouding the great legs. The flare tower gushed a vibrant flame of burning gas into the night.

'Oh, it's beautiful,' Andrea breathed. 'It's magnificent. I never thought it would be like this.'

She had to share her wonder with someone but the only person near enough was Dr Duncan Hunter. She turned towards him, forgetting her tears, her face glowing.

CHAPTER TWO

ANDREA felt a quiver of excitement as the Lochinvar rig drew closer. Below was the icy North Sea, dark like steel, fathomless, choppy and erratically malicious, the waves glimmering with reflected light from the rig.

Conversation was impossible, but she shot a glance of triumph towards the taciturn doctor.

'You'll never make me leave,' she said.

'I give you fourteen days,' he said, lip-reading to some extent. 'You'll be begging to be taken off.'

She shook her head in disbelief. She was not prepared for the sheer size of Lochinvar, its workover mast like a giant's finger pointing to the sky. There were three decks, or modules, with utilities, accommodation, control centre, helideck and a wellbay module with the working facilities for the well. It was like something from a Steven Spielberg film. She half expected green, seaweedy alien beings to emerge and greet her. A myriad legs and steel columns supported the platform, going deep down into the sea.

By now Andrea had become used to the noise and motion of the helicopter and she appreciated the perfect landing the pilot made on the plate-sized helicopter deck. As the aircraft steadied on the deck, Andrea wondered how she was ever going to find her way round the jumble of construction buildings. She was going to be lost half the time. It was a hive of activity, roustabouts and rig workers hurrying about in their colourful overalls and hard hats. The rig was manned by two twelve hour shifts, so work never stopped.

Put on hard hat, Andrea reminded herself before she climbed out.

'Hard hat,' said Dr Hunter. He did not help her down.

'I know. You don't need to tell me.'

'Put it on, then. I don't want you out like a light with concussion for my next patient.'

She struggled to pull her bag out of the hold, keeping her annoyance under control. Now she had to report to the toolpusher, who was the drilling foreman and drilling boss, a man called Pete Overton. But before she could even ask the way to his office, a tall, swarthy red-haired man was pushing through the crowd, asking for her.

'Sister West? Thank goodness you've arrived. We've got an emergency on our hands and you're just in time. One of the divers is trapped.'

'Trapped?' Andrea was taken aback. 'Where? Shall I be able to get to him?'

'He's twelve feet below the surface. He was replacing a temporary patch on one of the legs when the patch suddenly collapsed and low air-pressure sucked his arm and shoulder into the hole. He's pinned underwater to the rig structure.'

Andrea summoned all her courage. Her first patient was twelve feet under the water. She had never been underwater in her life apart from jumping into the deep end of a swimming-pool, but now it looked as if she was going to have to learn fast.

'How is his breathing?'

'So far, so good. There are two other divers in the water with him keeping him supplied with oxygen.'

'I'll need to see what there is in sick-bay,' said Andrea, running her mind over what she would need. 'Then if you could find me some scuba gear. . .'

'Get it in my size,' said Duncan Hunter, interrupting. 'Have you ever scuba dived before? No, I thought not. You would be more of a hazard than a help. I'll go down instead.'

Pete Overton looked relieved. 'I didn't know you were staying on board, Dr Hunter. I know we'll get the diver out now you're both here.' He gave some orders for the gear and beckoned Andrea towards a stairway. 'I'll show you the way to sick-bay and surgery.'

'I'm going to do this,' said Andrea to the tall, authoritative doctor, casually unzipping his survival suit. 'I'm prepared to go down in the water.'

'I admire your courage but you'll be useless, Sister West. Just what do you think you could do? Were you also prepared to do an underwater amputation?'

Andrea almost stumbled on the metal tread of the stairway as the shock of his words brought home the danger, and she privately accepted that in this case her inexperience really would be a hazard. Duncan caught her arm and pulled her close just for a second. The lapel of his leather jacket was rough against her cheek but she straightened up quickly and pushed him away. He chose not to be pushed and kept his grip on her and his nearness did not help to restore her sense of balance.

'Careful,' he added. 'It's a long drop. We haven't time for a woman overboard as well.'

His grip slackened and Andrea hurried after Pete Overton, determined to put a distance between herself and the overbearing doctor. She must not make a single mistake in this, her first case. He would be down on her immediately, pointing out her unsuitability for the post again, humiliating her in front of the crew.

The sick-bay and surgery were on the second deck near the accommodation and recreational areas. There was not much time to look around, but Andrea was immediately impressed by the up-to-date equipment and spotless cleanliness. The previous medic had obviously been a perfectionist, for she found everything she might need already packed in an emergency bag.

'Might I suggest you change into your boots? Those sneakers are why you slipped,' said Pete Overton. 'And don't forget your earmuffs.'

'Thank you.' It was the first kind word she had heard that day and she smiled at him. He seemed unnerved by her smile and backed off. Careful, she warned herself. Pete Overton might have difficulties.

She was escorted out on to the walkway that lead to one of the five enormous columns that held up the platform. The sea was pounding below and Andrea was careful not to look down. Vertigo was not something that had ever bothered her before, but it was bothering her now. A great deal of activity was going on and she recognised the powerful figure of Dr Hunter in a diving suit, being lowered into the sea. She shuddered at the thought of what he might have to do in that murky water. . .

'What are they planning to do to get the trapped diver out?' she asked. 'Cut a bigger hole?'

'No. They can't get him out that way because of the conflicting pressures inside and outside the column. So the welders are going down inside the column to try to weld a metal tube over the diver's arm. Then they'll pump water into the tube through a hose to equalise the pressure. It ought to blast him out.'

Andrea shuddered at the thought of the man being blasted out of that black water. This was certainly a long way from the A & E department at St Jude's. She thought of the brave men down there desperately helping their workmate. Lucas could not have done it, Lucas with his well-cut suits, his tidy administrative office, his softened hands. She had once thought those hands were magic. . .she must have been mad.

'I hope it works. It sounds bleak.'

'They'll never give up. They're a great team.'

It was hard to see what was going on despite the floodlights on the scene. Andrea clung to the walkway rail as the wind buffeted her. She was beginning to understand why Dr Hunter thought the rig was too dangerous a place for a woman. It was one thing to work in the safety of the sick-bay and quite another to have to cope with the appalling weather outside.

She was already bedraggled, her mass of dark coppery hair escaping from the hard hat. Her anorak was wet and her corduroy trousers soaked. She should have put on her waterproofs but there had not been time. Rain was trickling coldly down her neck like ice splinters.

And down there in those murky depths was a man trapped by the arm. And another man prepared to undertake tricky surgery if that was the only way of saving a life. She had to admire the doctor's cool nerve, though there was little else she liked about the man.

'Is this a really bad storm?' she shouted.

'Heck, no, Sister, this isn't a storm. This is plain, ordinary rough North Sea weather. Fairly normal. Wait till you see a real storm. We batten down the hatches and stay inside.'

Suddenly they heard cheering as the water broke and the diver was brought to the surface, supported by the two other divers and Dr Hunter. The complicated metal tube and controlled pressure had blown him out of the hole.

Andrea moistened her lips as they carefully raised the diver on to the widest part of the walkway then carried him back on to the platform. He was having trouble breathing; his suit was singed from the welding, his arm mangled and his chest crushed. She removed the bulky helmet and listened for breathing with her ear over his mouth and nose. There was a bluish-grey tinge to his face and his chest and abdomen were not moving.

She did not hesitate. She placed him on his back after cleaning out any obstructions from his mouth with a clean dressing. With a handkerchief over his mouth, she began artificial respiration at once, knowing that every second counted.

She blew steadily and slowly into the diver's mouth, keeping his nostrils pinched. She gave the first dozen inflations quickly and noted with satisfaction that the colour of the face and lips was beginning to improve.

A dripping figure went down on his knees beside her. He ripped off his helmet and his dark hair clung wetly to his head. The man looked exhausted, grey-faced. Suddenly she wondered how many hours he had been up and working.

'No hand compression if possible,' said Duncan Hunter. 'He's probably got chest injuries.'

Andrea nodded. 'I guessed,' she gasped between breaths. 'Crushed chest. . .mangled right arm.'

'He's starting to breathe. Good, well done. Let's raise him to a half-sitting position, leaning over to his injured side.' She could have sworn that his gravelly voice was fleetingly kinder, but the concern was for his patient, not her. She looked at the doctor quickly; his tough face gave nothing away.

The diver was coughing now and groaning, his face pinched with pain.

'We'd better get him to hospital as fast as possible. There may be internal injuries but he might get away with a few fractured ribs.'

'I'll make him as comfortable as possible,' said Andrea. She put some loose padding into the armpit and supported the arm using a triangular sling. Then she tied the arm to the body using a narrow folded bandage below the area of chest damage. They made a temporary stretcher with a blanket, rolled tightly at two edges, with six men to carry the patient up the awkward stairways to the helideck.

'Sorry, mate. I can't give you any morphine for the pain. It'll only increase your breathing difficulties.'

'That's OK, Doc,' the diver gasped. 'What's a pain. . .friends. . . Hi, Sister. . .you're. . . improvement on. . .last medic. No grey beard.'

'I'm working on it,' said Andrea, hiding a grin.

The diver was being carefully borne towards the helicopter which was waiting on the helideck. Dr Hunter turned to Andrea with a basilisk stare.

'Well, Sister, you certainly fix a mean bandage, but wait till you've a corneal eye burn or a chancroid to deal with. Then maybe you'll change your mind.'

Andrea hoped she would not have to deal with a surface eye burn or a soft genital ulcer. She could not meet the air of toughness he exuded and felt faint with shame.

'Don't worry, Dr Hunter; I can cope with both. And if I'm in trouble, I'm sure you'll come winging out to my assistance. It's such a comfort to know that you are at my beck and call. I promise not to call when you are involved in any recreational or leisure pursuits.'

'Such consideration will be appreciated. I don't like being bleeped halfway up a rock-face.'

'Or halfway through a night out?'

'I don't remember when I last had any time off,' he snapped. 'In fact, I don't remember when I was last in bed. We had a multiple pile-up last night. Kids death-riding in a stolen car. When will they learn? I had to pick up the pieces and try to sew them together again.'

'Kids. They think it's just a lark.'

'I understand you've volunteered to take on being entertainments officer while on the rig. A secret Redcoat under that starched bib? I should warn you that you won't be here long enough to organise a round of bridge.'

'You're wasting your time,' said Andrea. 'My contract is watertight.'

'I'll find something in the small print. Your appointment was made without consultation with me and I'm sure that if it came to a showdown, ColPet would prefer to let you go.'

'You mean, you'd put your own job on the line?' Andrea was astounded. The gaunt doctor looked perfectly serious.

'It is not a personal issue, Sister West. I'm sure you are an excellent nurse in the stable environment of a hospital. But. . .'

'But what?'

'I have noticed that you are somewhat highly strung and that might affect your doing the job properly. It could jeopardise the safety of the crew.'

'Highly strung!' Andrea fought to keep cool and

calm but the rising tone of her voice betrayed her feelings. 'Sure, I was nervous about the helicopter flight, my first. Sure, I was thrown by your brusque attitude in your surgery. You didn't exactly put out the welcome mat. I was tired and I had rushed north because I was told it was urgent and——'

'You're talking too much. Another sign of instability.'

Andrea clamped her mouth shut. She knew he was partly right. Her emotions were in a turmoil. Her father's unexpected death was still so recent and Lucas. . . How long did it take to get over an affair?

'You should get some sleep,' she said, trying to sound professional. His dark brown eyes were boring into her as if trying to see the woman within. 'Do you want something to help?'

'I don't take medication, Sister. Perhaps some tender loving care would be more therapeutic,' he said, but he was not looking at her any more. He was staring into the distance.

'Not in my contract,' said Andrea trying to control her surprise. 'Not even in the small print. But my personal feelings towards the male race won't stop me from being professional in my work and caring for all the workforce on this rig.'

The rig did move. It was something that Andrea was not yet used to. The catwalk was exposed, battered by the wind. A sudden gust caught her

off guard and she fell against him. He caught her
swiftly.

His lips touched hers, moving slightly before
they settled on her mouth with a warmth and
need. Andrea was shocked. She recognised
hunger when she met it. The good doctor was
starved of love. She knew a starving kiss when it
took over her lips. He was finding solace and
momentary oblivion in her feminine body, in her
softness, in the scent of her skin.

His arms closed round her and she too found
comfort in his nearness. Stop, stop; this is another
madness, said her mind, but her body did not stop
to think or care. It was the warmth of another
human being and for a few moments she allowed
herself to take all the pleasure there was to be
found in his kiss. It took away a little of the pain.

It was not a seeking, probing kiss, no sexual
overtones. But it was a tender kiss that had
Andrea melting as his persuasive mouth encour-
aged her to relax and enjoy every moment. She
sighed and curled against him, still aware of the
rough weather, her eyes closed against the bright
lights of the rig that stabbed the outer shadows,
and she let his body shelter her from the wind.

'Perhaps now I'll sleep,' he said huskily.

'It was also very foolish,' said Andrea unsteadily, surfacing slowly, her breathing ragged.

'Not so foolish, Sister. A kiss to soothe your
strung-up nerves; a kiss to put me to sleep. And

that kiss told me a lot about you. Don't worry, it won't happen again. You'll soon be on your way home.'

She was stunned, hurt that even after that lovely kiss he was coolly suggesting that she would soon leave.

'You'll never get another chance to find out anything more about me. From now on, I'm off-limits.'

'Please keep it that way.' He nodded. 'I don't approve of medics whose mind is not one hundred per cent on their work. By the way, you have been allocated one of the nicer outer cabins for the time being. I've made sure you don't have to share. Medics need to be able to get their sleep.'

'Am I supposed to be grateful?'

'You could try.'

'OK. I'm grateful. Thank you, Doctor.'

Andrea wanted him to go. His presence was too disturbing. She wanted to phone her mother from the radio room; she wanted to shower, unpack; there were a hundred things to do.

'Our patient is aboard the helicopter. You'd better hurry. I'm sorry that you still have another night's work ahead of you. But before you go, I think you should know that your bedside manner is sorely outdated. And I know more about tender loving care than you'll ever learn in a hundred years. I can see that you are a brave, courageous doctor, but as a human being you need some lessons in basic kindness and compassion.'

She heard his angry intake of breath and she knew that she had gone too far. But she had to say these hard things as a kind of protection for herself. It was verbal armour. She did not want a rerun of Lucas. And that kiss had stirred her womanhood, made her realise what she was missing, what she wanted, all the feelings that were dormant and waiting to be re-awoken.

'Don't forget to radio if you need me.'

'I won't need you. I'm quite sure of that.'

He strode off into the darkness and then reappeared by the whirlybird. It shattered Andrea to realise that she liked the shape of him: his tallness, the broadness of his shoulders, that wind-blown hair falling straight over his eyes.

She deliberately did not watch the helicopter taking off. She went the wrong way several times before she found the camp boss, Tom Groves, a plump, beer-bellied and cheerful individual who was in charge of catering and accommodation. The accommodation was regulated by grading and Andrea found that she had indeed been allocated a carpeted single room with a shower cubicle, toilet and washbasin, a writing desk, television and tea and coffee making facilities. It was not big but she was surprised by its comfort and luxury. She knew that the roustabouts shared rooms with three other crew-members, so she was being pampered.

It did not take long to unpack but for the second time she was so glad that she had put in those two white coats. When surgery opened tomorrow morning at eight, she was going to be the sister-in-charge and no one would doubt it.

She took stock of the floating city that was to be her home before turning in for the night. The food in the canteen was excellent and the menu more varied than she had expected. It was some-one's birthday and the chef had even produced a cake. The leisure area had billiards, table-tennis, and a supply of videos, but there were still a lot of men sitting around, doing nothing, idly smoking and creating a thick grey haze, thumbing through old newspapers and magazines. Andrea could see that being the entertainments officer could become a full-time occupation, despite Dr Hunter's snide remark.

Sleep did not come easily, as she was uncomfortably aware of the noise factor and the strange bed. All the sleeping accommodation was soundproofed but that did not completely cut out the noise. As she drifted into a restless sleep, she reminded herself to check the noise levels. She knew there were decibel limits and she'd seen workers not wearing earmuffs or even earplugs.

Dreams came and went like clouds but the face in them was indistinct. In the last months it had always been Lucas, suave and handsome, taunting her, cruelly exposing her love. . .but now another face swam into focus. . .dark, gaunt, and mysterious. The memory of that haunting kiss would not go away and she longed to feel his mouth on hers again. She pressed her face against the pillow, her lips quivering at the hopelessness of that longing. She would never let him kiss her again. . .never. She could never trust her heart again to know how to behave.

She was not prepared for the number of patients who turned up the next morning at her surgery, and not just out of curiosity. Spots. So many of the men had spots. It could be funny if it were not so serious. Big, grown men worried about spots.

Andrea dug her hands in the pockets of her white coat. Her blue jeans were fashionable and her navy check shirt neatly tucked into a wide belt, but she felt like an off-duty sister in them. Her hair was plaited high on the back of her head, the intricate braiding a work of art. But once the white coat was on and scissors and pen in the top pocket, her RNR pin in her lapel, she felt that she could face all those curious male eyes.

'I can't go ashore in this state, Sister. Look at my face and hands. It's the plague. I can't see my girlfriend looking like this. She'd run a mile.'

'Don't worry,' said Andrea. 'The spots'll disappear as soon as you return to shore. Believe me.

It's the oil-based mud you're handling. I can give
you some special soaps and effective shampoos.'

'But will they work? She'll go right off me,
looking a right prat.'

Andrea did not laugh at the young man's dis-
tressed expression. 'She won't go off you if she
loves you.'

Dermatitis and eye injuries were high on her
list of patients. Dermatitis was one of the most
frustrating problems for the crew. It was a permanent hazard. The skin became contaminated
with the chemicals used and erupted into ugly
spots. Andrea was not keen to prescribe one of
the potent steroid creams, since there were side-
effects. She referred one man to the company
dermatology specialist when he was next ashore
since he had psoriasis which was being aggravated.

Eye injuries were frequent, mainly because the
workers forgot to wear the required eye protection. There were different types of eye protection
and they should know which kind best fitted the
job. That morning she removed paint debris from
eyes that should have been wearing goggles, chip-
ping weld from a welder who should also have
been using a face shield and treated a flash-burn
in a case where dark safety glasses had been
ignored.

'I can see you've forgotten your safety procedures,' said Andrea as she bathed his eyes in
cold water.

'They feel all gritty,' said the welder, obviously very sorry for himself. 'And I can't stand that light.'

'I'm not surprised. You've got what they call arc eyes or welder's flash and that's not meant to be a joke. It's the ultra-violet in an electric arc which causes a kind of sunburn on unprotected eyes. Sorry about the bright light, but I have to see what I'm doing.'

She searched his eyes carefully for any foreign bodies, staining the area with fluorescein.

'Shall I go b-blind?' He was a man of nerves, his gnarled hands plucking at his jeans.

'Of course not. It's only sunburn on the surface of your eyes. Cold water, cold compresses and dark glasses for several days will help. Get Pete Overton to give you some other work until your eyes have completely cleared up.'

Andrea applied some chloramphenicol ointment and told the man to come back every four hours for further applications.

'On the dot, Sister Mae,' he said, adjusting the dark glasses rakishly.

Sister Mae? Andrea looked puzzled till she remembered her surname. This was obviously going to be her nickname on the rig.

'Pretend you're James Bond in those glasses, but no welding till your eyes have fully recovered.'

Andrea wrote up her reports. She would have to check if ColPet were providing enough protection gear then find out why the men were not using it. Often it was simply that they needed constant reminding, needed re-educating on safety factors.

The morning went quickly and Andrea was pleased that the work had gone so well. The men were quick to tease her, but on the whole their attitude had been one of respect. It was that look of vulnerability and gentleness that brought out good feelings. She reminded them of their families, of their daughters, of girlfriends left behind.

'Sister, can you come? Accident on the drill floor.'

Andrea grabbed her emergency bag, hard hat and earmuffs. Where on earth was the drill floor? She hoped that someone was going to show her.

'This way, Sister. It's his hand. A roughneck, cut by a spinning wrench on the drill floor.'

'Roughneck?' said Andrea, hurrying after her guide.

'That's a floorman who handles the lower end of the drilling pipe.'

The noise was horrendous, even with earmuffs, and everywhere dirty from the drilling mud used. How could men work in such hell?

The roughneck was holding his hand, white-faced, shocked and in pain. He was a big man, built like a gorilla. The hand bones were fractured in several places and one of the fractures was open. She knew that fixation in a straight splint

was only possible for a short time. The man
needed to go ashore urgently. That meant she had
to radio for medical assistance.

She put a crêpe bandage around the wrist to
support the injured hand and strapped the fractured fingers to the only good finger, making sure
that she did not prevent the joints from moving.
She put a dressing on the open wound and padded
the whole area before putting his arm in a sling.

'You'll have to go to hospital,' she said as she
gave him the standard antibiotic treatment. 'I'll
radio for help.'

She hated the thought of having to contact Dr
Duncan Hunter so soon, even professionally. He
was the last person she wanted to speak to. Yet
her heart longed to see him. She despaired of her
feelings, so out of control, so wild, so abandoned
when it came to this strange man.

CHAPTER THREE

DUNCAN HUNTER was turning up on Lochinvar almost every day. It was beginning to drive Andrea mad. She could almost sense the arrival of the helicopter and knew that within minutes she would hear his gravelly voice talking to someone just outside her surgery door.

'Dr Hunter. Another unplanned visit? I don't need you checking on my work,' said Andrea as her last patient hobbled out, a sprained ankle securely strapped. 'I can cope. You seem to regard me as a cross between a probationer and a total idiot. It hardly helps my standing on the rig if you show such a lack of confidence in my ability.'

'Did I say that I was checking on your work?' he said, roaming the confined space like a caged bear, curbing his endless vitality, his eyes taking in every detail. 'This is a purely social call. I'm on my way to another rig.'

'Then it's hello, goodbye, Doctor,' she said, gritting her teeth as she wrote up that morning's reports. 'I'm sorry you can't stay for a coffee. The other rig will be needing your urgent attention.'

'Not yet,' he said smoothly with a gleam of

satisfaction. 'I can stay for a coffee. My next patient isn't going anywhere. He's incubating measles, I suspect, since his two young children have both had it recently. By now there should be plenty of Koplik spots in his mouth.'

'Will you take him ashore?'

'I doubt it, unless there are complications, say bronchitis or a middle-ear infection. He's better off in isolation on the rig. As for your standing on Lochinvar. . .you've nothing to worry about. Jeff Knightly, the radio operator, tells me you are very popular.'

'The radio room is a hive of ridiculous gossip,' said Andrea, feeding instruments into the steriliser with a kind of ferocious determination. 'But I suppose that's also upsetting you. . . The men have accepted me as a professional medic. It doesn't worry them that a woman is in charge of the surgery. The female staff are overjoyed, I can tell you. At last a sympathetic ear that really understands their problems and will talk to them.'

'Don't try that one on me. I haven't changed my mind,' he growled. 'Your appointment is not yet confirmed. ColPet are looking into it. The first battering from a storm and you'll be blown overboard. And what about when you feel ill? What happens then?'

'I don't believe I'm hearing this.' Andrea's normally serene face was tense. She had thought that the job was secure, that the pay-cheque would go regularly into her bank account. 'It's practically medieval. Times have moved on, Doctor. I'm glad that you know all about the birds and the bees but be assured, a modern working woman doesn't have time for off-days or the vapours or any other Victorian ailment.'

'No headaches?'

'Don't men get headaches? Not exclusively a female ailment. If you'll excuse me, I've two patients in sick-bay, neither with measles, but still needing my attention.'

'Oh, yes. I heard. Stomach upsets.'

Andrea could barely contain her annoyance, keeping rein on an uncertain temper. 'How do you know everything? Are you spying on me? I suppose you have an informer on the rig. Is someone relaying back to you every damned thing I do and say?'

She could not keep the hostility out of her voice. To discover that she was being spied on. . . it was horrendous. She felt like complaining to someone high up at ColPet. But she did not want to stir up trouble. She wanted this job. She needed to keep it.

Duncan backed away, his hands up in mock surrender, his eyes glittering. 'Hey, hold on, Sister. Not guilty till proven guilty. As you said, the radio room is a grapevine and the news filtered through to me quite innocently. So I might as well have a quick look at them while I'm here, with your permission, of course.'

'Just as you wish,' she said, exasperated. She lead the way into the small white-walled sick-bay where both beds were occupied. The men looked up sheepishly, then exchanged alarmed glances. Andrea reassured them with a smile.

'Dr Hunter is just rig-hopping. He'd like to give you the once-over, to be on the safe side. Mike and Dud both have all-over abdominal spasms of a mild nature. Their temperatures and pulse-rates are normal. A mild form of gastroenteritis due, I think, to their bringing on board some sort of dubious, probably contaminated food. I've put them on a restricted diet and salt tablets in fluid.'

'Have you tried magnesium trisilicate compound five hundrd mg?'

'Of course I will if the symptoms persist. But they are settling down with simple treatment.'

'OK, own up. What was it?'

'Curried chicken kebabs. . .'

'We bought them on shore.'

'Isn't the food here good enough for you?'

'Just fancied them, Doctor. Don't fancy them now. I'll never touch 'em again.'

Andrea had to smile at their wan faces. 'I'll speak to the chef and see if he can't put chicken kebabs on the menu on a regular basis.'

'Have a heart, Sister. . .'

She poured out drinks of squash, checked their

charts of fluid intake, and straightened the bold
check counterpanes on their beds. 'I think you'll
live to see another curry,' she said sweetly.

'Don't even say the word, Sister Mae.'

Duncan Hunter followed her into the canteen,
chuckling. 'So you are collecting fans,' he said,
filling a coffee from the dispenser and handing it
to her. 'A few sweet words and those tough men
are your slaves.'

She was taken back by his sudden conciliatory
tone and the polite offer of a drink. 'Naturally.
It's part of my hidden charm.'

She took the coffee from him and waited while
he filled another plastic beaker. She hated drinking from plastic. She was going to bring back a
pretty bone china cup and saucer for her room.
There were several things she wanted to buy. Her
first hitch was nearly over and she would be
relieved in two days.

A whole fourteen days off. . . The prospect was
exhilarating. She'd heard nothing from ColPet
about terminating her contract, so she was pre-
suming that her entitlement to two weeks off
stood. She would have to find somewhere to live,
perhaps rent something cheap. She did not want
to stay in a hotel. This time she would not fly
south to see Florence. It was more important to
save the money. But she would phone; oh, yes,
she would phone her mother every day.

But since Duncan was on Lochinvar, Andrea

decided to pick his brains. She straightened her white coat, dug her hand in her pocket.

'I can't seem to make any headway with two problems. Slightly indelicate, but I can't seem to find solutions for insomnia and chronic constipation, apart from the usual pills and laxatives.'

'Both an oil rigger's plague, along with those damned spots. They're caused by stress, noise and lack of exercise. Medication is not the answer.'

'I know that. I also know what causes them, but I can't seem to do anything to change things. Exercise is almost impossible. I run on the heli-deck every morning but you can't get the entire workforce running.'

'I'd run with you if I were here. Every morning. You could count on it,' he said casually.

His words hung in the air, a promise as intangible as crystal drops. Duncan was looking at her intently with an unexpected wistfulness, and what she had been going to say vanished from Andrea's mind. She went completely blank. She did not know where to look. The man filled everywhere with his height and his presence, radiating health, confidence and an irritating masculinity, those dark brows drawn together.

Andrea struggled on, refusing to acknowledge the merest suspicion of a twinkle in the depth of his eyes. 'Their diet is good, plenty of fibre, fruit and vegetables on the menus every day. But do

they eat it? I don't know. I can't monitor what
they eat at every meal.'

'Will you have dinner with me next week?
Plenty of fibre, fruit and vegetables, of course. I
want to apologise for doubting your ability,
Andrea. It hasn't made me change my mind about
women medics on rigs, and I intend to get you
replaced by a man as soon as possible. But I admit
you are good at your job. Perhaps I could persuade you to work at my hospital. We're short of
a good sister in A & E.' He smiled down at her.

'You ask me out to dinner with one breath, and
then in the next say you're kicking me out of my
job? Oh, that's nice, Dr Hunter. Excellent timing.
Am I supposed to be overjoyed?'

'I'm offering you a shore job.'

'I want to work on the rig. I'm getting used to
it.'

'Perhaps I can persuade you over that dinner.'

'No, thank you.'

Alarm bells were going off in her head. It had
begun like this with Lucas. A simple meal after
working late together. Nothing special. How
could she have possibly known the consequences?

'Nothing on this earth could make me work in
your hospital, Doctor. Did you really expect to
soften me up with a little intimate dinner for two?
Heavens, what was it going to be, candlelight and
champagne?'

'No, haggis and whisky.' He stood boldly, legs

astride, thumbs in his belt, arrogant and unbending now.

Andrea felt the tension evaporate at the unconventional reply and she laughed. It was a soft and sparkling sound and Duncan was enchanted by it. He wanted to hear her laugh again. He wanted to say something really witty and original, but his wits seemed to have deserted him.

'Haggis and whisky? Do you call that a delectable and seductive meal? Brother, I wouldn't even cross the road for a sheep's stomach.'

'Duncan,' he said. 'But I'm talking about Glenhunter whisky, something special. How about a twelve-year-old malt straight from the cask?'

'Doesn't mean a thing. I prefer diet Coke.'

'That's disgusting. I can see your taste-buds need educating.' He was teasing her and it was a new emotion, funny, unthreatening. Perhaps that's what she needed. A little fun.

'Not that kind of education, thank you. Whisky is a menace to society. What about those kids who stole a car and crashed it? They'd been drinking, hadn't they?'

'They'd been drinking beer, not whisky, and a lot of it. Most whisky drinkers are connoisseurs. They take it very seriously. Well, is that meal on?'

She shook her head. 'I don't think it would be wise. I don't mix work with pleasure. Anyway, how could I enjoy it when I know that all the time you're trying to get me out of my job.'

He inclined his head stiffly, his eyes brooding. 'Let me know if you change your mind.'

'I won't.'

She threw her beaker into the waste-bin. She was regretting her refusal already. It was a long time since she'd had a proper date. It might have been nice to go somewhere civilised. Duncan Hunter was eating into her stone-wall resistance with his undeniable charisma and indefinable Gaelic charm.

Heavens, she could hardly even look at him; the longing was biting into her like a fearful ache. Hadn't she learned her lesson? One Lucas was enough in any woman's lifetime, she thought, clenching her hands. Her pride was slowly mending and she had no intention of allowing herself to be so stupid again.

'So how are your Redcoat activities coming on?'

It was a second before she realised what he meant. 'Very well, thank you. We've had a table-tennis knock-out competition and a bridge night. I got hold of a batch of new videos. They'd been watching *Star Wars* for three years. I'm hoping to organise a talent contest when I return. Everyone is rehearsing like mad in their off-duty time.'

'That sounds good. Are you going to sing? I notice that the men have found a nickname for you.'

She coloured faintly. 'With a surname like West, what else could I expect? And no, I don't intend to sing.'

'I certainly hope you'll come up and see me some time.'

'What a terrible joke! One out of ten for trying. And what do they call you, Dr Hunter?'

'Hawker. Not very original, is it?'

'Not original, but it fits. Built like steel and just as fast in the air. Audio-visual association.'

'Thank you for the coffee, Andrea,' he added politely. Andrea could see that he was looking regretful. Perhaps he really had wanted to take her out. He zipped up his leather windcheater and remembered that he had left his survival suit in her surgery.

She left the doctor to find his own way back. She didn't want to see him again. It was a flash-point situation. She wanted to be alone but she was sure that Mae West hadn't said that! A smile appeared and she suddenly felt much better.

Andrea liked the company of Pete Overton, the drilling boss, a pleasant and personable young man. But he was difficult to get to know, as if he was scared of women. He was hurrying towards her now, out of breath, his tanned face grave.

'Sister, thank goodness! An oxygen container has exploded. A roustabout's leg is burned. He was moving supplies. He's down by the mud tanks.'

'Give me two minutes. Spray the burn gently with a hose, fresh or sea-water. Don't remove any clothing. Get a message to the helicopter to delay their departure and ask them to wait. He will need to go to hospital.'

The youth's leg was a mess. Andrea's heart went out to him. His face was contorted with pain and he was clutching the top of his thigh. It appeared to be a second-degree burn with deep reddening blisters and weeping fluid.

'This is some shower,' he joked feebly as the water sprayed his face as well as his leg. 'Ouch.'

'It's cooling down the burn. What's your name?'

'Johnny.'

'OK, Johnny, relax. I'm just going to have a look.' Carefully Andrea tried to lift the leg part of his overalls but the fabric was stuck to the skin. There was little she could do except cover the burned areas with a dry, non-fluffy dressing when the hosing was over. She tried to give him a drink but now he was vomiting. He would have to have a saline drip.

A canvas stretcher appeared; her support team was getting well-trained and Andrea flashed a smile of thanks. Johnny was carefully lifted into it for transporting to the helicopter. Andrea scrambled after the team holding up the saline drip, holding on to her hard hat in the stiff wind, her pigtail flying.

Duncan spoke reassuringly to the injured roust-about as they loaded him on to the helicopter. But his manner to Andrea was cool and distant.

She remembered those last weeks at St Jude's, before she left. They had been a nightmare. Lucas had completely ignored her, not even acknowl-edging her presence at meetings. He had been the hospital administrator, hiring, firing, running the budget. Once she had told him it was all over, he had turned nasty, showing a side of his character that she had never seen before.

She had tried to pull her pride together but it hadn't been easy, seeing him every day, and she became skilled at hiding her feelings. *Damn* Lucas. She had just been another attractive female to bolster his morale and she had not found out he was married until it was too late, until she was disintegrating with love for him. She had tried hard to give him up, to believe what he said about his marriage: that it was only time before he would be divorced and he would be free. But it had all been lies. Never trust a man with smooth hair.

She pulled off her hard hat and the band on her pigtail, letting her thick hair unravel and blow across her face like a veil. She did not want anyone to see her looking so miserable. The blow-back from the helicopter swept her hard against

the rail, forty feet above the sea, but she didn't
care. Someone ducked her down. It was Pete
Overton, his strong arms hanging on to her.

'That was a close one, Sister. You nearly got
blown over.'

'Sorry, I was miles away. Not thinking. Thank
you.'

'You need a break,' he suggested hesitantly.

'It was a pretty rough night. . . Mike and Dud
were regretting their kebabs.'

She had not cried for a long time. She lay on her
bed letting the tears wash over her. Lucas, the
death of her father, and now the open disapproval
shown by Duncan Hunter increased her loneliness
and desolation. No one cared. It was hard to be
resilient in the circumstances when she wanted
comfort so much. Her body ached for someone to
cherish her shrivelled heart.

Her pillow was damp with tears. There was
nothing left for her but work. Pete was right; she
was very tired. It had been a busy hitch with the
crew bringing every saved-up ailment from dandruff to corns.

She forced open her eyes, knowing that she
must keep awake, and stared at the plain cabin
that was her home, the neat polished fitments, the
economy-sized shower, the empty book shelf. It
needed books, pictures, flowers, pretty cups and

saucers; she had to start putting her mark on the room. It was not supposed to be a prison.

Eventually she got up and splashed her face with water, put on a baggy red-striped shirt and plaited her hair again. She could not leave her two patients for long although she knew that the cleaners would be in sick-bay at the moment, chatting away as they polished.

The two men were dozing but she noticed a slight change in Mike's condition. He seemed to be holding himself rigidly whereas Dud lay in a relaxed position. She touched Mike's forehead; his temperature, which had been normal, was rising. That was odd. Her fingers moved to his wrist; his pulse-rate was rising, too. She did not like the change.

'Mike,' she said softly. 'How do you feel? Is the pain getting any worse?'

He nodded. 'Here,' he said, indicating the upper part of his abdomen. 'Hurts like hell.' He broke out into a cold sweat. His abdomen was tender, the wall of the abdomen rigid. It felt like a board.

'Do you get indigestion?'

'Yeah, quite a bit. More recently since I started on the rig. I've been taking things from the chemist.'

She gave him some sips of iced water and hurried to the radio room. Jeff Knightly, the radio operator, was sorting out a new delivery of paperbacks. He ran the rig library from the small radio room so he was never short of company.

'I need to contact whatever doctor is on call,' she said. 'Dr Hunter is already on his way back to Aberdeen. Is there anyone else?'

'I can make contact with the helicopter for you. Put these headphones on. What's the trouble?'

'Mike seems to be worse.' There was no point in hiding the problem. Jeff seemed to know everything. He probably knew the colour of her undies.

'Always stewed up about something, that bloke. Girl trouble most of the time and a different girl every hitch. He needs sorting out.'

'Well, it's not girl trouble now that needs sorting out.'

He was activating the call-sign. 'Hold on, we're getting through. . . This is Lochinvar. We have a medical emergency. Sister West wants to speak to Dr Hunter. . .'

Andrea moistened her lips. She did not want to speak to Dr Hunter but it looked as if she would have to. 'Dr Hunter. I think Mike has a perforated ulcer.'

'What are the symptoms?' His voice was totally professional despite the crackle of interference.

Andrea described the deterioration in Mike's condition.

'We'll fly out a Medivac to you. He needs to be in hospital. Give him fifteen milligrams of morphine intramuscularly at once with fifty milligrams of cyclizine lactate. If that doesn't help the pain, he can have another injection within the first hour.'

'Yes, Doctor. . .and standard antibiotic treatment?'

'Six hundred milligrams of benzyl penicillin unless he's sensitive to penicillin. Try him on a small amount of half milk, half water. Nothing else till he's in hospital ashore. And I want you to fly back with him. I'll send out a relief medic for the rig. A man.'

There was no mistaking the derisory tone of Duncan Hunter's remarks. He thought she had made an error in the original diagnosis and was withdrawing her services. Andrea felt that her diagnosis had been right at that time; she could not have foreseen a deterioration.

'Thank you, Doctor. Sorry to have troubled you,' she said coldly, handing the headphones back to Jeff. 'Thank you, Jeff, for getting through.'

'Don't worry. The Medivac will be here in no time.'

First she checked on her patients and did all she could to give Mike pain relief. She spoke to Tom Groves, the camp boss, about her room. Would she need to vacate it for the relief medic? He said he had spare accommodation so she could leave her things in it.

'I shall be back tomorrow,' she said firmly.

Duncan couldn't make her leave. He couldn't sack her. She had done nothing wrong.

'Too right,' he said. 'We can't do without you. You'll probably enjoy a trip to Aberdeen. See the bright lights, do a bit of shopping.'

'You must be joking. There won't be much time for bright lights or shopping.'

She had not expected to be taking another noisy helicopter flight so soon. The Medivac crew was fast and efficient loading the patient, and the changeover of medic was carried out without incident. He was a middle-aged nurse who flew regularly with Medivac on a locum basis and seemed pleased to have a change of routine.

'I won't kill off your patients while you're gone,' he said cheerfully.

An ambulance was waiting at Aberdeen airport and it whisked Andrea and the sedated Mike to the hospital. It was a big, functional, solid building made of local granite and she was again impressed by the efficiency that the staff showed. Mike was taken immediately to be X-rayed and a surgeon, whose name she did not know, was on stand-by.

Andrea strolled out of the busy entrance hall, feeling scruffy in her jeans, striped shirt and anorak. She was suddenly homesick for the activity of A & E and the comradeship of the medical team. It emphasised her isolation on the rig. She supposed it was too late to get transport back to Lochinvar. The helicopter shuttle would have closed down. She would have to stay the night in Aberdeen and fly back the next morning. Perhaps the ColPet offices would still be open? They might be able to provide some accommodation for her since she was still, on paper, working her hitch.

'I promised you dinner and you look as if you need feeding.' Duncan Hunter peered down at her as if she were another patient. He was hunched up in his leather windcheater, shirt collar unbuttoned, tie loosened, dark hair falling forward. He had had a heavy day, too, but her compassion only lasted a few seconds.

'Don't patronise me,' said Andrea smartly. She hitched her bag over her shoulder. 'I'm not a pet who needs feeding on time. Good evening, Dr Hunter.'

She turned briskly but found her way blocked by six feet of determined male, his mouth clamped into a line.

'I'm not interested in your feminist prickles,' he said. 'But I do know what would be good for you, both as a friend and a doctor. I took a look at your report book on the rig and your surgeries have been running at twice the normal number of patients.' His voice was razor-sharp.

'It's only initial curiosity. It'll settle down when they get used to me. Taking a vague ache and pain to the medic is a new leisure activity on the rig.'

'Curiosity because you are a woman, Andrea.

A novelty to the crew but time-wasting and expensive for the company. Another factor that no one seems to have thought of when they put you on the payroll,' he said darkly.

'I'm there, day in and day out. What does it matter whether I see three patients or thirty? Surely morale is more important and at least the men think that someone is taking notice of their small ailments, that they don't need to break a leg to get some attention.'

Duncan took her arm and began to steer her towards the car park. An ambulance arrived, lights flashing, rear doors already opening. The near-dark dusk heightened the sense of emergency and drama.

'All very commendable. But I suggest that we continue this discussion over supper. You look shattered and, as your doctor, I prescribe a hot bath, a decent glass of wine inside you and something light to eat.'

'All of which I can find for myself,' said Andrea, trying to shrug off his grip. But his hand tightened purposefully. 'And you're not my doctor.'

'So you know your way round Aberdeen, do you? Like a native? That's miraculous. I can just leave you here and you'll know where to go. Splendid, then I needn't worry about you any more.' He let go of her arm abruptly.

'I didn't ask you to worry about me.'

'No. And I don't intend to. That you look as

pale as yesterday's skimmed milk and can hardly
keep your eyes open is no concern of mine. But
the health of my team of medics and the workforce on ColPet's rigs is my responsibility. A
worn-out medic living on her nerves can't function
properly. Supposing you'd had a major accident
tonight, on top of a busy day. Half a dozen injured
in the moonpool area and needing urgent attention. What would you have done? Told them to
hold on a bit while you freshened up and took an
aspirin?'

'I'd have radioed for you,' said Andrea, stifling
a yawn. She was too tired for all this hassle and
wondered where she would find a bus. Duncan
was unlocking the door of a large old maroon-
coloured Jaguar XJ6. It was the four-point-two-
litre version and wore its age well. 'Could you
please drop me somewhere convenient in the
middle of town? I'd be grateful.'

'Right,' he said, sliding in and opening the
passenger door. 'I'm glad you're being sensible at
last.'

The car was roomy and comfortable. It was just
the kind of big, reliable car she would have
expected him to have. Dr Hunter would not have
gone in for anything flashy or too modern.

She had not realised how cold she had become.
No sweater, no gloves and only a thin shirt were
not enough now that the evening was drawing on.
Duncan started the car and switched on the

heater. She didn't care where they were going. He could hardly drop her outside the YMCA. Although, knowing him, perhaps he would.

She saw little of the city of Aberdeen as he drove through the busy streets. She glimpsed flowers everywhere and leafy parks and sturdy granite-built houses but her eyes were drooping and the warmth inside the car was making her sleepier. At least Duncan was not talking. She doubted if she would have been able to string two words together for a reply.

The car swept into a curved gravel drive flanked with trees, coming to a stop outside an old double-fronted grey granite house, its tall gables pointing darkly skywards, a columned porch covered in a wild tangle of wisteria.

'Wake up, sleepy-head,' he said, prodding her arm. 'I've brought you home.'

'Home?' She sounded like ET.

'My home. This is Hunter's Lodge.'

CHAPTER FOUR

DUNCAN steered her into a spacious entrance hall without waiting for any argument. There were plants everywhere, growing in terracotta pots, strong branches reaching up to the ceiling, white walls on which hung beautiful water-colours of the Highlands. White basket chairs with deep cushions were discreetly placed among the greenery. A few glossy magazines lay on low tables. It was like something out of one of those very magazines.

'This looks like a doctor's waiting-room,' she said uncertainly, moving about, touching things, looking at the watercolours with interest — seascapes and mountains.

'That's exactly what it is. I run a small private practice from home, when there's time. This way.'

He gave her no time to look around but began propelling her up the wide mahogany staircase and along a landing. Everywhere smelled of old-fashioned lavender polish. He flung open a door to a big bedroom that had a floor to ceiling bay window. Andrea felt instinctively that it had a view of the distant sea.

'You can use this bedroom and bathroom. There's no one using it at the moment. And there

67

are some clothes in the wardrobe if you want to borrow anything.'

Andrea wheeled slowly round the room, feeling that she was entering a film set and ought to take off her boots for the sake of the white carpet. A double bed was frilled with white organdie and satin bows like a wedding-cake and the curtains were a pale peach velvet that matched the upholstery of two armchairs. The wardrobe and dressing-table were made from Scandinavian pine, with simple, modern lines.

'Your wife has good taste,' said Andrea, her heart withering like an old apple. The double bed seemed to have no look of Duncan, no scent of him, yet there was room for two if they lay close. She should have known. No man as good-looking and successful as Duncan Hunter could have remained unmarried. He was too eligible. Doctors were always high on the marriage stakes. 'It's a beautiful room.'

He leaned his weight against the wall and watched her reaction. 'I don't have a wife. This room belongs to someone else.'

'You've no wife?' Andrea couldn't stop the words coming out with a surge of relief. But it was a woman's room; a woman who had lived with him and left?

'No wife, not even a small one. No woman would put up with my irascible ways and working hours and it's too late for me to reform. I'm thirty-eight and past redemption.' He waved his arm in the direction of the bathroom. 'Feel free. There's plenty of everything. I'll get some clean towels.'

The bathroom was a symphony of white and peach. There was enough shower gel and bath-foam to stock a shop. Andrea fingered them with envy and a peachy towelling robe that was hanging behind the door. She wondered about the woman who had last worn it.

She turned on the taps and poured in moistur-ised almond bath-oil. After nearly two weeks of showers on the rig, her skin felt dried out. She shed her clothes on the bedroom floor and stepped into the hot, fragrant water. 'Old prune,' she said affectionately to her face in the mirror.

As she soaped herself and let the water wash over her, she could not help remembering Lucas and his seductive voice. He had not thought she was an old prune. 'And I'll soap every inch of your silken skin. I'll pamper you in every way,' he'd said. But he had never pampered her. More empty promises. He'd always been in too much of a rush to have more than a quick shower on his own and get away. It was only later that she had found out that he had a home to go to, and a wife.

Andrea did not know now why she had put up with his ways for so long. She had been obsessed with the man, blind with love. And Lucas had known it, played on her emotions. He had used her. 'Get out of my head,' she said fiercely. 'I'm finished with you once and for all.'

As the water cooled, Andrea felt her eyelids becoming as heavy as lead. She must stay awake. It wouldn't do to fall asleep in the bath. . .

Duncan coughed discreetly. He was balanced on his haunches by the bath, a crystal goblet of white wine held unsteadily in his hand.

'A very nice hock,' he said, gazing down into the glass. 'Not too sweet but only slightly chilled, as I was not expecting a visitor.'

Andrea shot down under the water. 'Don't you ever knock?' she asked, her smoky eyes blazing furiously.

'Always—and I did. But you were asleep. I came in because I couldn't face a drowning in my own house. All that paperwork,' he said in teasing mockery. 'Don't worry, I didn't see anything through mountains of foam beyond a pair of knobbly knees, delightful though they are. Drink this, Andrea. Supper in twenty minutes, downstairs in the kitchen. Keep walking south.'

'You've got a nerve,' said Andrea, her mind in a spin. 'I've a good mind to leave.'

'OK, if you want to go. It's a long walk and it's starting to rain,' he grinned.

He left as abruptly as he had arrived, his back so splendidly tall and straight, the checked shirt straining across his muscular shoulders. His unexpected tenderness was more than she could stand.

She looked away quickly, sipped the chilled hock without thinking and found it delicious. It ran down her throat like mountain dew. She did not really want to leave. The idle threat had come out as an automatic response to Duncan's audacity.

It was far too late to wonder how much of her body he had seen and too late to worry. After all, he saw hundreds of female bodies in the course of his work. One more skinny one would make little difference, especially when he thought she was just a nuisance all round.

But she still covered her breasts and made sure that the door was closed before she stepped out of the bath and wrapped herself in the robe.

Her own clothes had disappeared. She padded across the carpet and opened the wardrobe doors, betting that the former occupant would be petite and willowy and nothing would fit. There was little to choose from, forlorn bits and pieces that would one day find their way to a charity shop. The woman had cleared out everything. Andrea took out a longish purple flowered skirt with a tie waist and a mauve top that hung straight to her hips. It was colourful and comfortable, if a bit long. She pulled her hair out of its plait and found that the steam from the bath had crinkled it like a Renoir beauty.

Except that Andrea knew she was no beauty with her heavy brows and strong jaw.

She used some moisturiser and black mascara,

and sprayed on a cloud of Estée Lauder's newest perfume, *Knowing*.

'And she left in a hurry. No woman goes without her perfume,' she murmured to her shocked reflection. She did not want to think of Duncan with this peaches-and-cream woman.

Now that she was ready, she could not find the courage to go downstairs. She did not have the strength or inclination for mental sparring with the determined doctor. But she was hungry. She could not remember when she had last eaten a proper sit-down meal. Did people still have meals with knives and forks and flowers on the table?

She went quietly down the stairs, resisting the temptation to open any more doors and peek in. There were at least six on this landing and some narrow stairs that must lead to the attics. It was a big house, full of ghosts and loving and living.

In the hall, she noticed a brass plate on a door: 'Dr Donnachadh Hunter' — his name in Gaelic — followed by an impressive string of qualifications. She did not know how he found time to do so much, hospital consultant, rig consultant and also a private practice. And who looked after him and this house? Who did the lavender polishing? There did not seem to be anyone around.

And which way was south? Her ears picked up a faint humming sound and she headed for that. She pushed open a door at the back which might lead to a kitchen area, and gasped in astonishment, then laughed at what she saw.

Duncan was standing bare-chested, his broad, sloping shoulders powerful and tanned, the dark hair thick on his chest and forearms. He looked magnificent and Andrea was taken aback by the disturbing effect he had on her composure. But it was not his physique which made Andrea gasp.

It was what Duncan was doing. He was holding up a navy shirt on a hanger, trying to dry it with the hot air from a hairdrier.

'Oh, Duncan, that's ridiculous. Don't you have any clean shirts?' She could not stop herself from laughing at him, caught at the empty, floating sleeves.

'Thank goodness you've used my name at last,' he said, heaving a sharp sigh of relief as he waved the drier in the air. 'I thought you were never going to get round to it. You can't keep calling me Doctor, especially when I'm cooking your supper. Yes, I'm out of shirts and there's no time to use the washing machine. I can't cook, either. Our supper is the only dish I can do with any degree of success. . .omelette.'

'An omelette will be fine. Can I help? You look as if you have your hands full.'

'You sit down and just look beautiful. That's all the help I need.'

It was a rambling, cluttered kitchen but with plenty of modern equipment. Duncan had laid the polished pine table with blue patterned china, the wine was in a cooler and there was a patterned china dish of peaches and kiwi fruit. He had whisked the eggs and a packet of prawns was defrosting on the counter. He poured her another glass of wine.

'This is no good for me on an empty stomach,' she said but drinking it just the same. 'I may get a little light-headed.'

'Ah, so you admit that you have not been eating properly?'

'Honestly, there hasn't been time. I'm lucky if I get a sandwich on the run.'

'So I noticed. That's why I brought you ashore a day early. You were near to collapse, young woman,' he said sternly.

'Why didn't you let me collapse, then?' she said drily. 'You could have let me fall about all over the helideck, clutching at rails, hysterical, becoming a public nuisance. . .a rig hazard, even. That would have suited your case, wouldn't it? Anxiety and mental illness are not unknown at sea. Then you could have packed me off home and replaced me with a sane and sensible male medic.'

Duncan stopped midway in pouring the egg mixture into a hot non-stick pan. 'Dear Miss Hospital Corners, is that what you've been thinking? Am I such a monster?'

'You made it perfectly clear from day one that

you didn't want me on Lochinvar. I did not enjoy being recalled. It was humiliating.'

He tipped the prawns on top of the sizzling liquid egg, tilting the pan, trying to do several things at once. 'You were not recalled, Andrea. Let's make that clear. I brought you back for your own good. You were at the end of your tether. I saw the way your hand shook when you took that coffee and as your doctor I diagnosed stress and overwork. You've probably been living on coffee.'

'You are not my doctor,' said Andrea sitting down with a jolt, the skirt billowing round her legs, then getting up again, unable to settle in his presence. 'Let's make that clear.'

'Yes, I am. Didn't you read your contract? Always read the small print. Now, don't let's spoil our first meal together, Andrea, with any more arguing. If you feel better tomorrow you can go back to the rig. I'll see that you get a seat on a shuttle. But first food and a good night's sleep. That can't be bad, can it?'

'Do you promise?' Andrea was still wary of him. She circled the kitchen table. She did not completely trust him. She could not be bought off with a glass of wine and a pleasant meal.

'I promise. Now eat up. Don't let this superb meal be wasted.'

'It won't be. You can certainly produce a decent omelette. It looks wonderful and I feel hungry.'

He shrugged himself into his now dry shirt and

buttoned it up. Andrea could not take her eyes off the glimpse of dark hair on his wrists at the cuff and at his throat. She felt boneless and pliant, weakening to touch those hairs, wistful to feel their silkiness.

He knew that she was watching him and he wondered if he had done the right thing, bringing this independent and spirited young woman to his home. But he felt he had to take care of her, even if it was only making sure that she ate and slept. Yet his own glimpse of her silken body at rest under the rising steam of the foamed water, so sweetly formed and girlish, had shaken him. She had looked so innocent and trusting, and he was appalled at his own wantonness in looking at her, longing to cup those curves, to feel them move beneath him. It would give him a blinding pleasure. He could not drag his eyes away from her soft skin.

'You've organised everything well so far,' Andrea went on as he folded over the omelette, then divided it on to two plates, as neatly as a surgeon would. 'Hijacking me from the hospital, cleaning me up, clothing me. So where do I sleep? Or is that all arranged, too?'

'I'm glad you've decided to stay. You have three choices. There's the couch in my consulting room, which is very firm and functional. Or you might prefer that fluffy meringue divan. My bed is the best.'

Andrea nearly choked on a prawn. Her crinkled hair fell around her face, hiding her embarrassment and her instant awareness of him. 'Are you serious?'

'No, I'm not. Don't worry, you are totally safe in my household,' he reassured her, wishing she weren't. He wanted nothing more than to carry her off to bed, make love to her and fall asleep with her curled against his side, the satiny smoothness of her shoulder very close. It would all be so natural. . .

'I'm glad about that,' she said, half sorry that she felt relieved. 'I'll take the meringue divan as long as the former occupant doesn't turn up in the middle of the night to collect her perfume. Although I'm not sure I can sleep in that room. It doesn't seem real somehow. . .more like a Hollywood film set.' She couldn't bring herself to ask about the woman who had slept there before.

'Not your style?'

'No, not really. I prefer something more homely.'

'No travel posters? Incense burning?'

'I don't know what I mean. I've never really had an opportunity to put a home together, never owned my own place. My mother had very definite ideas for our home at Hastings and my room was an ordinary schoolgirl's bedroom. Then I lived in various box-like nurses' residences of one sort or another. Now I've only a tidy, featureless

cabin. . .so I don't know if I have any taste.
Perhaps I haven't. I've never had a chance to find
out.'

Duncan saw an expression of despair in her eyes
and wished he knew how to remove it. He wondered if it was a sad love affair and if she would
ever tell him about it. Something was wrong; she
was so distant, remote from this world, for all her
outspoken ways.

He cleared the table when they had finished and
spooned coffee grounds into a percolator. The
colour was coming back into her cheeks and she
looked more relaxed, the pretty, flowing clothes
making her look so feminine. She tucked her bare
feet out of sight. The unknown woman had not
left any shoes.

'Let's take our coffee in the sitting-room. And
I've something special for you. . .a wee dram.'

'But I've told you I don't drink whisky.'

'This is different.'

He carried the coffee on a tray and Andrea
followed his tall figure, curious to see the style in
which he lived. The sitting-room was a big room
but it was very much a home with three sofas
placed round a low, walnut coffee-table covered
in books and magazines, a chess set. A fire was
burning in the grate but Andrea recognised that
they were lifelike gas-fuelled flames. The walls
were lined with bookcases filled with well-read
books and a grand piano was covered in silver-

framed family photographs. Duncan drew the long rose damask curtains which hung by patio doors leading out into the garden. He looked so different, a man at ease and comfortable in his own home.

She glimpsed another riot of flowers and shrubs in a long Victorian conservatory, its glass panes dark and silvery. Someone was a keen gardener. The night hung outside like a black-winged curtain, making the room seem cosy and safe.

'This is a lovely house,' she said.

'It's my parents' home. I've always lived here except when I was a medical student. I also spent several years serving in the Royal Navy, minesweepers.' His voice was full of pride.

'That explains a lot. A strictly male regime. You think you're still giving orders on board ship.'

Duncan shrugged his shoulders. 'I don't doubt it. The navy is in my blood and always will be. Just try this and tell me what you think of it.'

They sat at either end of a long sofa, sitting so that they faced each other. The space between them stretched like an ocean. So Duncan had been in the navy. She could imagine him in that immaculate uniform, perfectly at home on a huge bulk of floating steel. It was on the land that he was difficult. It explained the restless edge to his character.

He handed her a small glass of golden liquid. His fingers brushed hers and she drew back from

the *frisson* of skin contact. It was like an electric
shock. She could hardly think straight. The aroma
of the whisky was mellow, nothing sharp about it,
drenched in peat and heather and pure, soft
Highland water.

'It smells nice,' she agreed. 'What is it?'

'It's a twelve-year-old Glenhunter, the best
whisky for miles around. Just savour a few sips
and then take the last drop upstairs to bed with
you and you'll sleep well.'

He was dismissing her but suddenly she did not
want to go. There was a sort of milky silkiness
about the room that was soothing and peaceful.
The sound of the flames licked at the silence.

'Glenhunter? Do I detect another note of pride
in your voice?'

'You do indeed. The distillery is family-owned
and has been for years. It's one of the most
famous in Speyside, although it's not the oldest.
That honour belongs to Strathisla Distillery which
began working in 1786.'

'What makes it taste so good?'

'It's an ancient process,' he said with a wicked
grin. 'A secret not imparted to a mere doctor who
would not follow in the family footsteps. But I
believe it's all due to the wonderfully pure water
from the hill burns and springs.'

He breathed a short, ragged sigh as if reliving
old arguments echoing in this very room. There
had been such rows, and they had not been

reconciled before his parents had died. It was
something he deeply regretted. They had accused
him of abandoning the family business.

'So your parents built this house?'

'No, it's older than that. My grandfather built it
when he married my grandmother. They are all
dead now and the house belongs to me. My uncle
Angus and his sons run the distillery and they do
it very well. I'm an absentee director. I turn up
once a year at the annual general meeting, that's
if I'm available. They don't take kindly to my lack
of interest.'

'But your work is vitally important,' said
Andrea impulsively putting her hand on his arm.
He glanced down at her hand and she withdrew it
quickly as if stung. 'Don't they understand that?
You save lives.'

'Sometimes people think the family business is
more important, like continuing history. Perpetu-
ating the name, the reputation, something like
that.'

Andrea thought of her family and Florence's
worrying financial problems since the death of her
father. Neither of them had realised that he'd lost
a lot of money on Black Wednesday, had had to
take out a second mortgage on the house, and had
fallen behind with the repayments.

'Families can be the very devil,' she said,
scraping back her mass of hair, making her neck

childishly vulnerable. 'Sometimes their problems devour us, take over our lives.'

'Is that why you're here, Andrea? Working all hours of the day and night in a hellish environment? I thought it was for the money. . .yet you don't seem an extravagant person — no rings, no fancy jewels, designer jeans. Or are you running away from something. . .someone?' He looked at her intently, trying to fathom her sadness.

'No, of course not,' she said quickly, far too quickly. 'I'm not running away.' But she was running away, from Lucas and the hurt he'd caused, running away from herself.

'So it's worldly wealth, then?'

'I admit it is for the money. My father died recently. . .' Her hands were clenched round the whisky, white-knuckled. Duncan removed it. 'And he left his financial affairs in utter chaos. I can't understand how he can have been so careless. My mother could lose her home and she loves it so much, and it's all she has now. She couldn't move. . .'

She did not want him to see her upset but he had seen her trembling mouth and swiftly his arms went round her and they clung together, not asking those unspoken questions. It was too soon to revel in the joy of being in his arms, but she was suddenly nervous of being a woman, of where this warmth might lead. Duncan touched her hair with an awkward caress, her face, her lips so gently that she could hardly believe that it was the same man who had been bawling at her on the rig.

'Don't start crying. . .' he murmured and an unknown warmth began to kindle. No man had ever spoken so tenderly to her. 'I couldn't stand it.'

He began to kiss her, inhaling the fragrance of her skin, exploring the pearl-smooth secrets of her mouth. These were kisses that touched a raw desire that had lain dormant for a long time. A delicious ache coiled within her stomach, a gorgeous glow travelled through her veins, set fire to the core of her nature. She was greedy for his touch, longed to be crushed by the weight of his body.

She felt his powerful shoulders under her hands and moulded them, her fingers digging into his muscles. The moment stretched endlessly and her eyes shone with wanting him. Yes, wanting him. Yet how could she want him when she hardly knew the man? This was another foolish madness that she did not know how to stop. Her body knew she could fall in love with him even if her mind would not acknowledge it. Her feelings were gathering with such intensity, her blood clamouring, longing for the pleasure that she knew he could share with her.

He stood up, pulling her with him, his hands on her back, making their bodies fit together. Neither spoke, yet their kisses said everything. Now he kissed again, a deeper, passionate kiss, a probing kiss that dispelled all her fears. He was a prize for any woman with his gentleness and his passion, strength and tenderness. She would let happen whatever was fated to happen. She only wanted to be with him, in any way that he wanted.

'I want you so much,' he said, burying his face in the softness of her hair, his hands stroking the narrow curve of her hip. 'Tell me to stop, if I must, woman. But if I have to leave you alone, tell me now before it's too late.'

'Don't leave me. Yes, oh, yes, Duncan. I want you, too. I'm sure of that.'

He looked deeply into her smoky eyes. 'Such honesty from my sweet Andrea. Just what I would expect — total honesty. You would never lie to me, would you?'

'Never. There will always be the truth between us. No lies. I promise you that.'

He slid his hands up under her loose top and drew in his breath as he touched the bare skin of her waist. It was unbelievably soft and warm and inflamed all his senses.

'This is madness,' he gasped.

'Sshh,' she said, moving her mouth to his. 'Not madness. A kind of living, a kind of need.'

'Yes, a need, Andrea. I need you and want you, but only if you're sure.'

'I am sure. . .'

'Shall we go upstairs. . .?' He hung on her

answer, almost afraid of what she would say. She put her arms around his waist, hooking her thumbs into the belt of his trousers. She laid her cheek against his chest and breathed in the fresh, clean smell of his masculinity, felt the friction of hair against his shirt. He was all man and the pleasure of touching him was beyond belief.

He threw his arms round her shoulders and took her towards the door and the stairs, switching off the lights as he passed them. Their hips brushed as they climbed the stairs.

'Not this room,' said Andrea as they passed the door. 'In case she walks in. . .'

'I think she's in Sydney,' he chuckled, pushing open the door to his bedroom.

It was totally different, as she might have expected, a supremely masculine room, navy and alabaster, furniture of rich mahogany. Books everywhere, even on the floor. He cleared papers off the bed where he had been working on them and sat her on the navy duvet. He crouched in front of her, tentatively clasping her cold bare feet.

'Cinderella. Lost both her glass slippers,' he murmured, warming them with his hands and kissing her toes. The feeling was delicious and sent the most tantalising tingles through her body. She could not believe the intensity of the pleasure. The room was warm yet she was shaking with nerves. He drew her slowly against him and held her close, letting his hands roam, heat shaking through her body. How could this man produce such magic?

She was watching him intensely, her finger stroking the strong line of his jaw, the straight nose, the dark and heavy brows, wishing she could feel at ease. First times ought to be banned. These were strange, uncharted features that she longed to commit to memory, but he was already stroking her legs and finding the tied fastening of the skirt. He pulled away the folds of material and threw them on the floor into a purple pool.

She felt naked and suddenly insecure yet she was fully clothed down to the thighs. Her lacy blue pants were tiny, too flimsy, too frivolous. She wished she had on some plain cotton knickers.

He touched the hemmed edge of the scrap of lace and she jerked back as her skin was burned by a live wire.

'So the prim Sister West is not all starch and strait-lace,' he said, teasing her with affection, his eyes dark with desire.

Suddenly Andrea panicked. What was she doing, getting into another situation like her affair with Lucas? She could not fall in love with Duncan, must not repeat that mistake. This was madness, the same madness. She had to escape.

She sat upright, struggling to pull the top down to cover her pants. It wouldn't reach. She rolled over on the bed and leaned down to find the skirt, pulling it round her like a towel. She crouched back on the bed, shaking.

'I'm sorry,' she gasped. 'I can't. . .'

Duncan looked aghast. 'What have I done? What have I said? Andrea, please. . .tell me. I know I'm clumsy. Whatever I've done, I didn't mean it. Tell me what's the matter.'

His face was drawn, his body tensed, tormented with longing for her. Her sudden change of manner was a shock. Where had the soft and loving woman gone? An icy hand touched his spine as he realised that somehow he had blown it.

'I don't want to start anything. I'm sorry; it was a mistake. . .' she quivered, her feet hunting for shoes that she had not worn. 'I can't replace the woman who has left you.'

'Andrea. . .please. That isn't true. You're not replacing anyone. There's no one in my life.'

'You were laughing at me. . .'

He ran his hands through his hair, distraught. 'No, my dear. . .not laughing at you. Laughing with you and only in the kindest way, because I thought. . .I thought we were very close then, close enough to enjoy all the joys of making love and that includes some laughter. . . Oh, what the hell!'

He flung himself away, white-faced, his eyes blazing. He felt humiliated.

'Yes, a stupid mistake. I'm sorry I started

anything. I have paperwork to do and I shall be in my study. I hope you sleep well, with your prim, maidenly modesty intact.'

Duncan lowered his mouth to hers and kissed her hard and brutally, without feeling.

'Dream on that, Sister West.'

He pushed her away and strode out of the room. Andrea rocked back, her knuckles in her mouth, her bruised mouth parted in anguish.

CHAPTER FIVE

'STAY at Hunter's Lodge? You mean Dr Hunter's place?' Andrea was aghast at the news which the personnel officer at ColPet had given her. She had worked the last two days of her hitch back on Lochinvar and was now ashore for fourteen days' leave. She had called in at the offices to get help in finding temporary accommodation, only to be told that the Lochinvar medic was always allocated the flat in the coachhouse at Hunter's Lodge.

'That's ridiculous. I can't stay there,' she fumed.

'But it's a very convenient arrangement, I'm told. It's not easy to find rented accommodation in Aberdeen and prices are sky-high. It's very good of Dr Hunter to let us have this flat. . .'

'Oh, yes, he's a paragon of virtue,' Andrea muttered under her breath. It was a difficult situation. She had to stay somewhere. But their last encounter had been so distraught and shattering, she did not know if she could bear to see him again. So far she had avoided any contact. He had been detained at the hospital the last few days and a different doctor stayed in radio contact with the rig so she had not even had to speak to him.

She made up her mind. 'All right, just for tonight. Then I'll be out first thing tomorrow fixing up my own place.'

'That's a good idea, Sister West. Here are the keys. If you'd kindly drop them in when you leave.'

Andrea spent the day going round the estate agents and it was not long before she realised that finding a rented place was not going to be easy. The rents were horrendously expensive and even bedsitters were hard to find. She had a sinking feeling that she might have to settle for bed and breakfast in a guest house. And she knew what that would mean. Landladies wanted everyone out of the way after breakfast. She would be at a loose end all day, wandering the streets and the museums.

She trudged round the Crown Street and Great Western road area in a fine grey drizzle, but all the net-curtained windows were hung with 'NO VACANCIES' signs. The oil workers had taken every room, often sharing. By late afternoon she was tired of searching for somewhere to stay. She sat down in a steamy cafe and thankfully ordered a pot of tea.

The waitress looked sympathetic. 'Trying to find a room, miss?'

Andrea nodded. 'It's hopeless.'

'Needle in a haystack. You might have more luck looking out of town. The city is packed with

oil workers. You could try Stoneywood or
Bucksburn or one of the small places along the
coast.'

'Thank you,' said Andrea. 'I might well do
that. . .tomorrow.'

Since she did not know where she was and had
lost all sense of direction, she took a taxi to
Hunter's Lodge, apprehensive and laden with
doom. It was indeed a granite city, with so many
houses and municipal buildings built of the warm
watery grey stone, beautiful wide streets like some
foreign capital. And everywhere were lovely parks
of piercing green that she longed to walk in and
enjoy the delicate, rain dripping flowers. ColPet
had given her a tourist list of parks and even their
names were full of Highland music. . . Hazlehead,
Duthie, Cruikshank, Banks o'Dee. . .

But now she just wanted to sleep, to wrap
herself in unconsciousness. She had slept badly
the last few nights and hardly at all that night in
the fussy, frilled bed. When she got up the next
morning, Duncan had gone. She discovered a
housekeeper, Mrs Macdonald, working in the
kitchen, bustling and friendly, and she had made
Andrea some tea and toast.

'The doctor went very early,' she confided.
'That man works far too hard. He needs to slow
down or he'll be in an early grave. A lot of doctors
die young, don't they?'

'A professional hazard,' said Andrea gloomily,

still feeling distraught and having to force the toast down. She was upset that last night had gone so terribly wrong and she knew it was all her fault. She was scared of falling in love again, of being committed, of being hurt. For a moment Lucas had flashed back into her mind like the smooth-voiced devil he was and she had not been able to banish him.

She had thought that Lucas was firmly banished to the past, nothing more than a shadowy ghost. But she had been wrong. He had returned to spoil a special moment with more than a normal quota of male vengeance.

Walking down the gravelled drive was like an instant replay. The same sweeping branches hung over, ladened now with rain drops, brushing her face with wet fingers.

The coachhouse was some distance from the main house and Andrea saw that it was used now to garage cars. One of the double doors was open and Duncan's Jaguar was missing but there was evidence that a big car was normally garaged there. She went up a plain wooden staircase wondering what on earth she was going to find. She half hoped that it would be absolutely awful, wreathed in cobwebs and quite uninhabitable.

The stairs opened immediately into the loft of the coachhouse and a whole open expanse of gabled and beamed roof was above her, warm and ancient brown, only vaguely cobwebby. One end

was furnished with armchairs and a sofa, a desk
and wall bookcases, muted colours of burgundy,
brown and white. She turned and saw that the far
end was a sleeping area which was on a different
level and reached by two graduated steps that
stretched the width of the building.

Someone had furnished the flat with care. A big
bed was covered in a hand-stitched patchwork
quilt of blues and browns. One wall was fitted
cupboards. Blue rugs littered the polished floor.
She opened a door at the end and found a compact
bathroom and adjacent kitchen, so tiny she could
barely turn round in them. It was ideal. She would
love to stay here. If only it did not belong to
Duncan.

She zipped open her bag and put away some
clothes. She already felt at home, and decided a
cup of tea would complete her arrival. It did not
take long to discover that the kitchen cupboards
were bare. It was going to be a hot cup of water,
try to find a late night shop, or go begging to Mrs
Macdonald.

The light was on in the kitchen so Andrea
thought that the housekeeper must still be there,
perhaps making a supper for Duncan. He was not
home yet because the car had not arrived. At least
she would have some idea of his comings and
goings. Andrea hurried across the darkening
garden, rehearsing a little speech.

She knocked on the back door and opened it carefully.

'Hello. Mrs Macdonald? It's Andrea West. I only want to borrow a tea bag and a dram of milk.'

'Come in, Sister West. So you've met Mrs Macdonald, my treasure. One tea-bag and a dram of milk? Is that all? How about a digestive biscuit? Go really mad and have two,' Duncan suggested.

He was making a mug of instant coffee. He looked desperately tired, as if he had been up all night. His face was gaunt and his brown eyes almost unfocused. She was shocked by the change in his appearance. He was leaning against a wall as if he did not have the strength to stand straight, stirring his coffee endlessly, not drinking.

'Are you all right?' she said, her animosity forgotten. 'You look dreadful.'

'A long and complicated breech birth. Thirty-six hours,' he said in sharp bursts, as if he was beyond putting together a complete sentence. 'Mother with a heart problem, paroxysmal tachycardia. The paroxysms of rapid heartbeats were difficult to control during the labour. I thought we were going to lose her at one point. But once she saw her baby. . .'

'The old magic.'

'Yes, seeing the baby did her more good than any of my sophisticated medication. The heart-rate had reached a hundred and sixty to a hundred and eighty beats or more a minute. We could hardly find her pulse.'

'And the baby?'

'A perfect seven-pound boy. They are going to call him Duncan, of course.' A faint gleam of amusement touched his tired face, then vanished. 'There are a vast number of baby Duncans toddling around Aberdeen. Future historians are going to have trouble sorting that one out.'

A crust of silence settled on the kitchen, broken only by the ticking of an old clock. They were both remembering their wanton passion with pangs of guilt and embarrassment. They made an effort for normality, pushing the disturbing memories to the back of the mind.

'Ah, yes. . .you came for a tea-bag. Do you like the flat?'

'Yes, it's lovely.' Andrea could only be truthful. 'I like it very much, but I'm not going to stay. It's pretty difficult to find anywhere to rent in Aberdeen, but tomorrow I shall carry on looking further out, and as soon as I've found somewhere, I'll go.'

'That's ridiculous. Why not stay here? You don't want to add travelling to your problems.'

Andrea shook her head. 'I think the less we see of each other, the better. It's obvious that we don't get on and. . .' her voice faltered. She could not mention those kisses, those intimate caresses, his hands on her body. 'You obviously disapprove of my work and I don't want an argument every time we meet.'

'Don't worry. You'd hardly ever see me. I'm out early and back late. We could have a kind of signal, a shirt hanging out of a window perhaps. Then you would know if I was in or out.' It was difficult to tell if he was being sarcastic or funny.

'That isn't what I mean,' said Andrea, not amused. 'I am quite capable of saying a polite good morning to you, but it would work better if I were not here at all.'

'A complete break,' he said ironically. 'Nothing to remind me of your existence, or you of mine. Is that what you have in mind?'

'Exactly. It would be sensible.'

'Sensible? Is that how you put everything unpleasant out of your life? By simply ignoring it? Head-in-the-sand syndrome.' His irony was unsettling.

But it was not what she meant at all. Duncan was dead on his feet and all her womanly instincts told her to put her arms round him, tuck him into his bed and let him sleep. It was not love, it was compassion; the feeling that made her a good nurse and a caring person. All her patients felt it and responded to her warmth.

So why couldn't she show that warmth to Duncan now when he obviously needed looking after? She wanted to act naturally and follow her instincts but there was this inner caution warning her not to be trapped again. Her body would let her down once she was near him, touched him. She felt a shame accompanied by a fierce and hostile indignation. He was both man and adversary.

She expected to see some sort of triumph in his eyes but there was none, only the weariness. His shoulders were hunched as if he was cold and he was holding the mug with both hands to capture the heat from the hot liquid.

Andrea became all nurse, all professional. She put aside any thoughts of being intimidated by his authority or presence. This was simply a sick man.

'Have you taken your temperature recently. Duncan?' she asked, tea-bag forgotten. 'You don't look too good.'

'Of course I haven't. Don't start being bossy. I'm not paranoid about my own health. I'm pretty fit most of the time. It's just tiredness.'

'Mrs Macdonald told me that you overwork and don't stop to eat properly. You were lecturing me on the very same theme a few days ago, remember? Not very sensible, if I may say so. And it makes you a prime target for any infections going around.'

'Stop fussing. . .' he said wearily, passing a hand across his forehead.

'Will you let me take your temperature?'

'Will I heck!' he said, turning so abruptly that he spilt the coffee over his hand. Andrea took it from him and at the same time swiftly felt his wrist. He was hot. He was burning up. A faint gleam of perspiration seeded his forehead, as he said, 'Go away. Go home. Wash your hair or something.'

'I would suggest, Doctor, that you are feverish and should take the appropriate action. Like going to bed, like taking two paracetamol tablets, like phoning the hospital that you won't be in tomorrow.'

'Nonsense. Leave me alone. I don't need you to tell me what to do. I'm perfectly all right.'

'With that headache?' she said quietly, noting the way he was avoiding the light and had flinched at her voice. 'What makes you think that you are immune to influenza? Did you have the flu immunisation jab? We've four cases on the rig. It could be the start of an epidemic.'

'Spare me the lecture, Sister. I had my jab, or maybe that was last year. Take your tea-bag and be gone. I just want to be left alone,' he groaned with an abrupt, dismissive gesture.

He slumped into a chair and put his elbows on the table, propping up his chin with his knuckles. His whole posture was telling her to get out. He did not want her ministrations. If he was going to be ill, he preferred to be ill in solitude.

Andrea moved quietly round the kitchen, switching on the kettle in case she needed hot water for a bottle to warm his bed, finding herself a tea-bag and a small jug of milk. Duncan's supper was in the fridge, a plate of roast beef covered in film, waiting to be reheated in the microwave. Mrs Macdonald was indeed a treasure.

The silence grew between them. What was he thinking about? Had he sat at that big kitchen table doing his homework as a schoolboy? Had he argued round it as a teenager, putting the world to rights? This homely kitchen would be full of childhood memories.

With a jolt, Andrea realised that Duncan was right. She found it difficult to face anything that might be unpleasant. There were the months being romanced by Lucas when she had been afraid of losing him if she went home for a weekend. She had been a fool. If she had gone home, she might have been more aware of her father's illness, of his financial problems. Her throat ached with guilt.

'You need looking after,' she said carefully.

'If I decide I need looking after, I'll hire myself an agency nurse. At least they do what they're told,' he snapped.

Andrea was not going to be dismissed so lightly. She took a deep breath to quieten her uneven breathing. A small mutiny flowered beneath her denim shirt, strengthening her determination. She had coped with reluctant patients before now, though not one quite so tall and strong and argumentative. She doubted if she could lift him.

He went to the tap and filled a glass with cold water. The water splashed over his cuff. He did not seem to notice.

'I guess you're just tired,' she said, taking the opportunity to steer him towards the hall and up the stairs. She knew the location of his room only too well but she tried to think of nothing but what she had to do .

His room was in amiable disorder, clothes flung all over the place as if he had dressed in a hurry, the bed used as extra desk space. She restrained herself from comment, and instead quickly tidied away the papers and smoothed the lower sheet, plumped the pillows and made Duncan sit on the edge of the bed. Doing three things at the same time was fairly normal. She pulled off the hand-made leather shoes, the black silk socks, massaging the hot dry skin of his feet. He groaned and fell back on the pillow.

Perspiration like dew broke out on his forehead. Andrea wasted no more time. She unbuttoned his damp shirt and peeled it off him, manhandling his heavy body, heaving him against her to remove it from his shoulders. He was shivering now, his breath short.

'Go away, Sister Mae,' he moaned. At least he knew who it was. 'Leave me in peace.'

'It's no use you trying to get rid of me,' she said, unzipping his pants. 'You've got influenza and a hefty dose of it. Any aches or pains?'

'Back, legs. . .my head's pounding like a steam engine. . .'

She averted her eyes from his hair-softened chest, the flat stomach, the navy briefs tightly stretched over his hips and pulled the duvet briskly up to his shoulders. 'Then you won't refuse two paracetamol tablets every four hours until your temperature is normal.'

'Downstairs surgery. . .drugs cabinet. Keys in my pocket,' he said, giving in with a deep sigh of relief. 'Help yourself.'

'Your Glenhunter is safe.'

It was not how Andrea expected to spend the first evening of her leave but she was strangely happy. She sponged his hot skin, gave him plenty to drink, left him to fall into an uneasy sleep. She looked in frequently to watch for any signs of pneumonia, rapid breathing or a bluey tinge to the lips. But it seemed Duncan was having a sharp, unpleasant attack of feverish influenza, with no complications.

Andrea took the ignition keys off the hall table and managed to garage the Jaguar. Duncan had left it parked some way back on the driveway, unable to drive a yard further. She locked up the flat and went back to the house with an extra jersey. It was a truce for the time being.

She made a nutritious sandwich with layers of lettuce and tomato and slices of mature Scots cheddar; laid a tray with a mug of coffee and an apple. She took it through to the sitting-room with a selection of the daily newspapers from the surgery. It was a long time since she had managed a relaxed supper and in such a comfortable room. Why was it she felt so at home amid the friendly clutter of Duncan's house and in his flat? There was something unreal about it all. Still, she thought, stretching out her legs to the flickering flames, it was only for tonight. Tomorrow she would search for her own place.

She found a book on seabirds on the shelves and immersed herself in the dozens of species of gulls who pilfered her bird-table on the rig. Summer plumage, winter plumage, first winter, second winter. . .the birds changed their feathers as frequently as a woman. Cory's Shearwater. . . 'one has been seen off the coast of Aberdeenshire'. . . Andrea smiled to herself. She must take more notice of her feathered visitors.

Several times she looked in on Duncan, took him fresh drinks, medication, and let the fever burn itself out. He slept fitfully. Once, in the small bleak hours of the night, he caught her hand with fingers that were long and dry as she sponged his face and neck.

'Hey, what's all this in aid of, Sister?' he croaked. 'A change of heart? I thought you hated my guts.'

'So I do,' she said with spirit, drying him with rather more energy than necessary. 'And you deserve all you get. It's time you knew what your patients go through when they're ill; the best cure for arrogance is a taste of your own medicine.'

He spluttered on his drink which was a sign of some recovery. 'And your particular brand of tender loving care. . .is certainly a one-off experience, not to be missed. A cross between a Chieftain tank and a killer whale.' He sank back on the pillows and closed his eyes. But there was a twitch of humour around his mouth as if he was well satisfied.

'Make the most of it. This is me in a good mood,' said Andrea.

What she didn't know was where to sleep. She felt like Goldilocks — so many beds to choose from. But the feminine bedroom again did not tempt her and instead she took off her shoes and jeans and bedded down on the sofa with a blanket found in a linen cupboard. She slept well, despite waking to peer at Duncan in the pearly half-light of early dawn. His face, in repose, just missed being handsome, but his features were so strongly drawn that she was lost in contemplation of them.

It was all she could do to stop herself touching his sleeping face. The frown lines had disappeared, the dark brows were relaxed, dark lashes sweeping his cheeks childlike and appealing. His mouth was slightly open and she longed to trace the soft curves with her finger but she dared not be so foolish. She made herself stand up, her feelings in a state of unhappy confusion. How could she be so drawn to him when he admitted that he was trying to get rid of her.

Later she made a cup of tea in the kitchen and took it to the window to drink. It was raining again, a steady downpour that all but obliterated the overgrown garden. There would be no flat-hunting today if it continued. They would be marooned in the house, cut off from the world by the rain and a nasty species of rampant germs.

Andrea was not surprised when Mrs Macdonald phoned to ask the doctor if she could have the day off. Her path was flooded and she'd heard the bus services were up the creek.

'You stay at home,' said Andrea. 'Dr Hunter has a bad dose of flu and won't be going any-where. I'm looking after him. And you'd be better off keeping out of the way. It's very infectious and you don't want to catch it.' She did not add, 'at your age.'

'Are you sure you'll be all right on your own?' said the older woman, concerned. 'And the doctor? There's plenty of food in the larder and the fridge.'

'I can cope. It's plain, simple nursing. Though he's not exactly the ideal patient.'

'I can imagine.' Andrea heard a low cackle. Mrs Macdonald obviously knew her employer well. 'He always hated being ill, even as a small boy. Nothing kept him in bed, not even measles with complications. I'll be in tomorrow, the heavens permitting.'

So Mrs Macdonald had been around in the Hunter household for a long time. She was obviously very fond of Duncan and probably knew him better than most. Andrea could imagine that tough little boy resisting all attempts to restrain him, even in illness.

Andrea heard signs of activity from above and raced upstairs. Duncan was charging about, straight from the shower, his hair dripping, a towel slipping down his narrow hips. He stopped when he saw Andrea in the doorway.

'What do you think you're doing?' she glared, raising her brows in true Sister West fashion.

'Going to work. Any objection?'

'You're not going anywhere. Duncan, you're the worst patient I've ever had to deal with,' she said, sweeping another towel off the rail and dabbing at his damp-haired chest. 'Do you want to be really ill? You're asking for trouble, wandering about wet and half naked.'

'Don't argue with me. I'm going to work.'

'How?'

'By car, of course.'

'I've hidden the keys.'

'I'll phone for a taxi.'

'The phone lines are down,' she lied. 'We've had a storm while you've been tossing and turning all night. Look at the weather outside. It's a deluge. We'll be marooned for days.'

She hoisted the towel round his waist and anchored it with a deft twist. His virtual nakedness was unravelling her composure and her eyes ranged uninhibitedly over his glistening skin, travelling up and down his powerful muscles and long legs. Desire inflamed through her from head to toe, shaking her shadowy aloofness. Never in her life had she felt so wanton, yet so complete and fulfilled. Perhaps he was what she had been waiting for, someone like Duncan Hunter.

'I was hot and sweaty. I needed a shower. Or were you planning to give me a blanket bath, Andrea?'

He was better. She could tell that from the intent look in his eloquent eyes. But the ravages of the night were apparent. He did not object when she tidied his bed and pushed him back into it.

'Haven't you got any pyjamas?' she asked.

'Never wear them.'

She rummaged through the closet and took out a plain black cotton T-shirt, shaking out the creases. 'You'd better wear this in bed. I'll telephone the hospital and tell them you've got flu.'

'Aha! Thought you said the lines were down.'

She didn't answer that. 'Stay put. Breakfast is on its way.'

'What a bossy lady. I pity your patients. Those

oil rig workers must be reduced to jelly. A collective sigh of relief can be heard as far away as Fraserbourgh at the end of your hitch. I shall be doing everyone a favour when I recommend your removal,' he said affably.

'Are you still trying to terminate my contract,' she said, putting a thermometer in his mouth to stop the flow of words. She had raided his surgery. 'I'm staying put and no one, not even you, is going to take my job away from me. What gives you the right to put me out of work? I told you, my father left a lot of debts and I need the money.'

'I'm going to offer you a job at my hospital. Safer, more suitable. I told you I'm desperate for a good sister in A & E,' he said, whipping the thermometer out of his mouth. She put it back firmly, looking at him with icy disdain.

'Will you never learn? I'm not leaving and not even you can make me. Your temperature is down and pulse-rate is normal. I'll fetch you some breakfast, if I can stop myself from putting something unpleasant in your orange juice. A strong dose of castor oil perhaps.'

'Tut, tut. Not used any more, Sister. Keep up to date with the latest medication. Castor oil went out with the end of the work-house.' His amused eyes followed Andrea as she turned to leave.

Andrea calmed down in the kitchen. Duncan was just seeing how far he could taunt her and she refused to have any sense of her own worth eroded by his mockery. It was little enough these days.

She prepared a light breakfast. . .juice, toast and honey, weak tea. It was still chucking it down, the rain enveloping the house in a dull grey shroud.

'Not out flat-hunting?' he asked as she came in with the tray. 'Thought you couldn't wait to get away from Hunter's Lodge. The devil's harem and all that.'

'I've no intention of swimming round Aberdeen. It'll have to wait till the weather clears. Mrs Macdonald isn't coming in.' She hesitated. 'May I use your telephone? I was lying when I said the lines were down. I'd like to call my mother. And I did promise. . .'

He looked aghast, a piece of toast and honey half way to his mouth. 'Andrea, why didn't you say so earlier. Of course you can phone your mother, any time.'

'You were ill last night, feverish. . .' she said, taken aback by his sudden change of manner. 'I could hardly ask you then. . .'

'Such devotion to duty,' he said laconically. 'If I were not still racked with pain. . .er. . .everywhere, I might easily leap from my bed and give you a big sticky kiss.'

Andrea retreated at speed in case he carried out his threat. As she left his room, she heard low husky laughter turning into a cough that spread a coverlet of warmth and contentment through her body. The man was a menace. The sooner she distanced herself from him, the better. Her feelings had been dormant; now they were shuddering on the brink of ecstasy. But she did not want it. She would rather remain out of his life.

CHAPTER SIX

THE fourth flat that they looked at was even worse than the previous three. The estate agent had not mentioned peeling paint, damp unlovely walls, inadequate cooking and heating facilties. Even the view of other backyards was dismal.

'You can't live in a place like this,' said Duncan, slamming the door on the converted garage. 'It's hopeless. Why don't you give in and use the coachhouse at Hunter's Lodge? You know it makes sense.'

Andrea also knew it made sense but she was not ready to capitulate yet. Duncan was over his bout of flu and itching to get back to work and it was only by agreeing to his offer to drive her around that she had managed to extend his convalescence by one day. He had been a difficult patient but even he admitted that her skilled nursing had made life easier.

'We've looked at a converted hayloft, a room over a fish shop and a bed-sit which could only be described as an up-market hen house. When are you going to give in, Andrea? It all seems ridiculous when there is a perfectly good flat waiting for you at Hunter's Lodge. Why won't you stay there?'

He opened the door of the XJ6 Jaguar and Andrea slid in her long legs. She could not tell him why. She couldn't tell him that she was being drawn more and more to the taciturn doctor. It was not good news. She had no intention of becoming involved with any man again.

'We should argue every time we met. I don't want to spend every leave coping with a problem neighbour as stubborn as you. In fact that converted garage might be a haven of peace and quiet. I could get on with my life and you could get on with yours.'

'Don't worry. I have very intention of getting on with my own life,' he said, throwing the car into gear and backing out of the side turning. 'You keep out of my way and I'll keep out of yours. We need never see each other. Except when you radio for my help, which no doubt you'll find yourself having to do frequently.'

Andrea gritted her teeth. 'I'll only radio for you when I need you. But I can't stop you dropping in like some nanny who can't take her eyes off her charges. If you want to add to your workload then that's your business.'

'Good. Then that's settled. We can stop this farce of looking for a flat for you and go back to Hunter's Lodge for what's left of the day. Right?' His glare almost melted the windscreen. His thick dark grey polo-necked jersey almost obliterated his chin, but it jutted firmly over the rib.

'I suppose so.' She knew she sounded ungracious and tried to remedy the fact. 'I admit the flat is very nice.'

'So it ought to be. It used to be mine when I was a student. I made it my haven of peace and quiet where I could study and have my friends back. There's been a few all-night parties, I can tell you.'

'I hope that there are no all night ghosts,' said Andrea, visions of lovely girls flitting everywhere. 'I don't want any reminders of your misspent youth.'

'All delightful memories, Sister.' He grinned. 'Nothing to bring a blush to your maidenly cheeks. You can sleep chastely in the bed of my youth.'

'Your past is no concern of mine,' she said sitffly. She looked out of the window and saw that they were leaving the knitted rows of suburbia behind. 'Where are we going?'

'I'm taking the coast road. It's the long way round but I thought a breath of fresh air would do us both good. Do you fancy a walk along the beach?'

She nodded, suppressing a surge of pleasure. She loved walking by the sea. 'That'll make a change. I don't often see the sea, do I? Novelty factor plus. Doubt if I could recognise the stuff. Waves or something, isn't it? Let me know when we're getting there.'

The coast was beautiful, sands sweeping a long

washed line, fringing the bay like cream lace. It might be the worst sea in the world for weather but at this moment it looked magnificent, the grey-green waves pounding the beach with high, powerful curves, their music a crashing crescendo. Andrea slipped off her shoes, pulled off her socks, and rolled up the hem of her trousers.

'Coming for a paddle?' she shouted, running down to the sea, her hair flying.

'What about my delicate state of health?' He pointed to the region of his throat and chest and coughed.

'I said paddle, not swim. You can keep your clothes on.'

'Thank you. I thought I was taking off my clothes the other night, before I was ill. I got it all wrong, didn't I?' His eyes held a depth of meaning that she barely understood.

Andrea was surprised at his honesty. But she wanted to talk about their lovemaking. She wanted to tell him of her uncertainty, of the torments in her mind.

'I am so sorry, so very sorry, Duncan,' she said. 'I am sorry about the terrible hurt. But I was so uncomfortable. . . I mean, not ready. Yes, I wanted you very much. . .physically I wanted you. You are a very attractive man.' She faltered, her heart twisting painfully at what she had to say. 'But mentally I wasn't ready. There has to be love with lovemaking. . .for me.'

'And there had been another love and that still hurt?' Duncan was so perceptive.

'Yes. I made a fool of myself. A big mistake. . .it's all regrets now. But I ended it before it hurt anyone else.'

She had not hurt Lucas's wife. She had stopped seeing him, but he had been always there, in the hospital, around every corner. It was nearly a year now. A year of anguish.

'Thank you for telling me. I thought it was something I said.'

Andrea gave him a sweet smile. It *was* something he had said but she need not tell him. 'I made all sorts of arrangements for my mother before I left,' she said, changing the subject.

'You're a good daughter,' he said with an odd look.

'Not all the time. I'm no paragon.'

'I'm relieved about that. But I've less enthusiasm for icy cold water. Watch out, you'll get frostbite.'

'It's wonderful,' she said, throwing her arms about in abandoned childhood ecstasy. He had never seen her look so happy and he did not know why. Andrea knew why. She was going back to Hunter's Lodge and she would be near him every day even if they did not speak. The wind streamed through her hair, blowing away the cobwebs. All the hassle of the last few days was tossed to the sea and swept out to the far ocean. For the first time she saw the sea as a friend and not an enemy. It sang a secret song to her and she almost heard the words.

She walked backwards on the wet sand so that she could watch the activity on the cliffs. Noisy seabirds clung to the narrow ledges, raising their families, declaiming territory.

'I hear you feed the groupy seagulls on the rig,' said Duncan.

'I knew you had a spy watching me,' she said, still treading backwards, digging in her heels. 'That proves it.'

'So you like seabirds?'

'Yes, I like all birds. They are just plain greedy and don't pretend to be otherwise. There's a lot of wasted food goes overboard; I just scrounge anything suitable from the kitchens and make sure the birds get it.'

'You're just a big kid.'

'It doesn't cost anything.' Andrea winced at her trite words. It sounded as if she was money-mad and she wasn't.

'Waste not, want not. Eighteenth-century proverb,' Duncan said, catching her hand. It was a casual gesture but her hand felt so right clasped in his. She did not pull away but splashed through the baby wavelets with him in companionable silence.

'I always come down here and walk by the sea when things are getting difficult,' he went on. 'All my life, the sea has been a refuge, a listening board, my *papaver somniferum*.'

'Your what?'

'The seeds of the poppy plant, age-old pain-killer and opiate. Waves are less addictive.'

'Are things difficult now?'

'Nothing I can't handle. But there's this awkward young woman on my staff who insists on doing a man's job when clearly she should be safely ashore, spending her evenings flower arranging and doing crochet.'

'Perhaps she hates flowers and finds crochet boring. You shouldn't try to organise someone else's life.'

'Impossible. All women like flowers.'

'Women like being given flowers, but they don't necessarily enjoy sticking wobbly stalks into wet lumps of Oasis.'

They were nearing a beached fishing boat and a cluster of people milling about on the sand, sorting and winding lengths of wet net. They heard a cry of pain and a figure sank to his knees, clutching his arm.

'That looks like trouble ahead,' said Duncan, breaking into an easy run. Andrea stumbled over the sand, her trouser legs wrinkling down round her wet ankles. They reached the group of fishermen and went immediately to the stricken man. He was a big, burly chap, sleeves rolled up, and in his forearm was a big messy hook.

Andrea flinched. She was not that squeamish but she had never seen a hook in a man's arm before. It reminded her of paintings of medieval torture. She swallowed hard.

'OK. Don't panic,' said Duncan. 'I'm a consultant on the rigs. I know what I'm doing.'

The fisherman's skin was reddened and swollen and the fish hook was embedded in the fleshy part of his forearm, seeping fluid and blood.

'Does your first-aid box have any cetrimide solution?' he asked. The crew looked at each other, bewildered, and Duncan muttered under his breath. 'Obviously not.'

'I'll get soap and water from the galley,' said Andrea, climbing aboard. She knew he wanted to clean the area around the hook. The hook would be infected from the bait.

Duncan found a piece of strong thin line and put it round the shank of the hoop and slid it down until it touched the skin. Andrea could hardly watch him. He pressed the eye of the hook carefully down with one finger until it was nearly flat with the skin.

'What are you doing?' she whispered.

'This is the way to detach the barb from the tissues,' he said. 'At least, I'm hoping so. I don't get too many of these to do.'

'So ye tell me now, Doctor,' said the fisherman, his swollen face grey with anxiety. 'Jest get it out. Anyways ye like.'

'Hold this down, Andrea,' said Duncan. As soon as her finger was in place over the eye of the hook, he pulled on the line sharply. The hook came out of the wound through the point of entry, tearing the skin but not the flesh.

The man breathed a big sigh. 'Gi'ed me yer hand, Doctor. Would ye like a wee dram? I know I would.'

Duncan shook his head. 'No, thanks, mate. We'll just get this cleaned up and put on a dressing. Then you ought to go to a hospital for an antibiotic. You could get a nasty infection. And while you're there, ask someone to look at that rash. You're probably allergic to curly weed.'

The fisherman nodded. 'Aye, drives me mad,' he said, scratching.

Andrea and Duncan walked back to the car. 'That was pretty neat,' she said, knowing she could not have done it.

'Beachside surgery,' he said. 'And did you notice his skin? It's a dermatitis caused by contact with some seaweedy stuff called curly weed. The backs of his hands and wrists are badly affected.'

'Yes, I saw his skin was weeping, itchy and cracked. And is that the same condition on his face?'

'Yes, that swelling round the eyes is conjunctival inflammation.'

'What can they do for him?'

'The best treatment is to remove him from all

contact with curly weed. He could change to deep-water fishing. They'll give him chlorpheniramine four milligrams and hydrocortiscone one per cent ointment for the skin.'

'Betamethasone and neomycin eye-drops for the eyes?'

'Right on, Sister. Ready for some lunch?'

'We'll go dutch,' she came right back.

'Chinese or Indian but not Dutch. Aberdeen has every kind of ethnic eating except Dutch. I feel hungry for once. Your light diet was becoming a little monotonous.'

'I'm a nurse, not a cook. Count yourself lucky I gave you anything to eat at all. I was tempted to let you starve.'

'I want to show you all of Aberdeen,' he said, enthusiastically waving his arms. 'It's a splendid city and there's so much of interest. People down south don't realise it's such a great place. I want to take you to Her Majesty's Theatre to see a show, to Cove Bay in the south which is an old Kincardineshire fishing village, walk the Bridge of Dee when there are millions of daffodils in bloom and carpets of crocuses.'

'Hold on, hold on,' Andrea murmured.

'We could drive to the western Grampian, to the waters of the Moray Firth. You'd love the forests and the rivers full of salmon and the coastline of fishing villages.'

Andrea found herself wrapping his enthusiasm

around her, soaking up his words and the spell of his gravelly voice. Promises, promises. Her heart was racing and she tried to restore a sense of balance, of common sense to the conversation. All this togetherness threatened to engulf her. He couldn't mean it. It must be some devious ploy to soften her up.

'If you get your own way, I won't be here in the spring for the crocuses,' she pointed out.

'There are forty hospitals throughout the area of Aberdeen. Any one of them would give you a good job, especially mine. And the Royal Aberdeen Children's Hospital won the Hospital of the Year award in 1989. Doesn't that tempt you? But don't let's spoil lunch. I want to thank you for giving up your leave to nurse a crotchety and ungrateful patient.'

'I could hardly leave you to burn yourself out.'

'Where would you like to eat? Somewhere old or somewhere new. There's Ardoe House, an elegant old country house with turrets and towers, all open log fires and magnificent views of Lochnagar. Or do you fancy the modern Waterside Inn, gourmet restaurant and a swim afterwards in their leisure pool?'

It was a meal she would never forget. No candlelight or champagne, but magical just the same. Andrea hardly knew what she was eating, dimly remembered spicy home-made broth, fresh salmon from the river, a delicious fruit flan. And afterwards they took their aromatic coffee in the red wallpapered lounge, sitting on deeply cushioned sofas in front of a log fire. It crackled a fiery message.

She could imagine for a few delightful moments that they really meant something to each other. That Duncan cared for her; that this was the beginning of old-fashioned courting. He was everything she had ever wanted in a man. Lucas faded forever from her mind, and definitely from her heart. Sunlight bounced off the polished surfaces in the room and the fragments of crystal brilliance made everything seem unreal.

Duncan's bleeper brought them both back to earth. She had not realised that he had reactivated his bleeper after lunch.

He left to make a phone call. When he returned, he was already getting out his wallet.

'I have to go,' he said, asking for the bill. 'Sorry about this, Andrea. I knew it was against all probability that I could take a whole day off.'

'Drop me at the hospital. I'll find my own way back to Hunter's Lodge.'

'I'm not going to the hospital. The call was from the shore radio station. There's a small fishing vessel adrift, damaged and only just afloat, probably rammed; three survivors on board, clinging to the structure. They need a doctor and medivac out there fast. I'm going straight to the heliport.'

'Shall I come too?' said Andrea. 'Three survivors. . . I could help. . .that is, if there's room on board for me?'

'No. You'd only be in the way.'

'I thought you'd say that,' Andrea fumed. 'You know it's nonsense. How can you cope with three people, maybe injured, maybe contamination with oil, dehydration, malnutrition, all at the same time? Advanced state of torpor. . .have you got three pairs of hands?'

Duncan looked at her keenly and she found his expression hard to read. It was the detachment of a medical scientist. He was in a solitary world of his own, assessing her ability, not seeing her as a woman who had once lain restless and seeking in his arms.

'No, it's too dangerous.'

Wild colour flooded her cheeks. 'I could use a very rude word,' she said. 'But I won't. I'm too well brought up and civilised. But you really make me mad, Dr Hunter. What makes you think it's any less dangerous for you? Please think again. You may need my help.'

She said it all with unconscious dignity and grace. Duncan accelerated along a clear patch of roadway, not seeing the windblown verges or rose bushes scattering their petals like confetti. The minutes were running out. He did not have the time or the stamina to spend on more argument. The flu had left him drained of strength. He admitted to himself that he might need her toughness and her expertise.

'Pilot and winchman. You and me. Three survivors, prone. That's seven.' He was muttering to himself. 'I guess there'll be just about room if you don't move about. And I suppose I might need your help. Get a survival suit on as soon as we get to the heliport. Check the medical supplies on board while I go to the operational room. We'll need extra dry clothes, blankets, hot sweet tea, plastic bags, thermal wraps, soft cloths and strong paper towels for any oil. Are you warmly dressed?'

Andrea shook her head. Her brightly coloured cotton sweater and jeans were not enough. It would be very cold out at sea and in an exposed helicopter. 'Not really. . . I came out dressed for flat-hunting.'

'There's a wool jersey somewhere on the back seat. Put it on.'

'What about you?' she said, struggling into the dark blue, overlarge hand-knitted seaman's jersey. She wondered if Mrs Macdonald had knitted it for him.

'I can pick up a waterproofed crew sweater with our survival suits. I may have to be winched down.'

A chill settled on her composure like a cold hand. Duncan could be hurt, dangling on the end of a wire like a puppet. But at least she would be there, doing everything she could to minimise the danger. This rescue was going to be teamwork, difficult and dangerous, but she was glad to be going with Duncan. At last she felt truly alive. She was going to get a chance to prove her worth and ability. All three survivors would be suffering from hypothermia, and at different stages. She went over the stages in her head. . .excitation stage, a dynamic stage, torpor, apparent death.

Conversation aboard the helicopter was impossible because of the noise but Duncan passed her his set of notes. It was important to have every bit of information to make an assessment of the seriousness of the situation. The sea below was wild and stormy, troughs and crests of waves quilting the darkly grey and murky depths. Even the thin skin of the helicopter was buffeted by the wind and she could feel the cold despite the bulky survival suit. Andrea shuddered at the sea's hostility. It was called the worst sea in the world and she was beginning to believe it.

At first it was only a dark speck bobbing on the ocean, lost from sight with each huge wave. A tiny bit of flotsam.

The fishing vessel was being tossed about like a broken toy. The pilot wheeled the helicopter round with the utmost skill trying to rendezvous overhead. The winchman slid open the door and the sudden gust of cold air took away her breath. The sound of the rotor blades and the pounding seas was deafening. Below, lying on the deck in awkward shapes, she could just see the men. They looked in the last stages of exhaustion and were probably unable to help themselves.

Andrea could not take her eyes off Duncan as he followed the winchman down to the stricken fishermen. She loved him so desperately and the thought of something happening to him was an agony, yet nothing would stop him from going down. She held her breath as the more experienced winchman guided the swaying doctor onto the moving shell of the shattered deck. She watched him examining the men and strapping the most seriously injured man into a Neil-Robertson stretcher so that it was impossible for the patient to slip or fall out.

The pilot gave Andrea instructions for keeping the winch wire from fouling any part of the ship or the rigging, her hands protected by rubber gloves.

It was the longest part, watching the stretcher being slowly winched up, spinning in the wind, their patient helpless in a canvas parcel.

She hauled the man aboard, unstrapped him carefully, sent the stretcher back down a secured wire to the vessel. The casualty was only a boy, already unconscious and in an advanced state of torpor with muscle rigidity and dilated pupils. The respiratory rate was slow with only three or four movements a minute. Andrea would not even hear a heartbeat with a stethoscope but she knew

the boy was not dead and he was capable of
breathing on his own. It was serious hypothermia.
Slow rewarming was essential.

Andrea made sure the airway was clear and he
was breathing. She enclosed him carefully in a
plastic bag with a blanket all round, ensuring his
head was covered and he was out of the draught
from the open side.

Duncan came up on the winch with the second
man. His face was beaded with sweat and spray.
He was feeling the strain, aching from the strength
needed to hang on.

'This one's got frostbite,' he said. 'He went in
the water to pull out his mate. It's his hands. But
he is conscious so wrap him up well and give him
some warm sweet tea and deal with his hands.
How is the other lad? I'd better take a look at
him.'

'Breathing very slowly, rate only three or four
a minute. Warmed slightly now from twenty-eight
degrees up to thirty.'

The second youth's hands were hard and with a
waxy pallor. But there was hope. If the skin had
died, it would have gone black.

'Can you move them? Try wriggling your fingers. What's your name?'

He shook his head with marked shivering, his
teeth chattering. He was very confused and
excited. 'Dugie. I'm Dugie. No, I can't feel a
thing. Will I lose my fingers? How's my mate?

What's the time? I'm meeting a girl this evening. Can I get a message to her? It's important. She'll think I've stood her up.'

'Don't worry, Dugie,' said Andrea, holding the warm tea to his mouth. He drank eagerly, spilling it down his chin. 'Tuck your hands under your armpits like this and let your own body heat warm them. It has to be done slowly. You were very brave to go in after your friend.' She wrapped him in thermals and blankets, keeping him out of the wind too. The inside of the helicopter was beginning to feel crowded. She and Duncan were almost climbing over each other, both chilled yet sweating at the same time.

Dugie's feet were also white, numb, cold and slightly swollen. She removed his wet canvas trainers and raised his feet, wrapping spare clothing round them. If she warmed them too quickly they would become very painful.

The winchman was guiding the last stretcher case into the helicopter, swaying on the wire like a trapeze artist.

'This one has had a slight argument with an oil drum,' he joked, but it was no joking matter.

The poor man's face and hands and clothes were covered in sticky black oil, his hair spiked with the stuff. Andrea cleaned the area round his mouth and eyes but could not remove any of his clothes until he had warmed up. They'd put him under a warm shower in hospital as soon as his body temperature was up. She used the paper towels and soft cloth to remove as much of the excess of the contamination as possible.

She managed to help him drink warm tea through a bent straw, wrapping him up in thermal wrap and blankets.

'Don't worry,' said Andrea. 'There's special jellied cleansing agents which will get this stuff off your skin, and with time and patience, ordinary hair shampoo will remove the oil out of your hair. You'll soon be as handsome as ever.'

The young man groaned, half-choking on the fumes. 'I ain't no Mel Gibson anyways.'

The two men struggled with the sliding door, forcing it to close against the pressure of the wind. Andrea held her breath, tensed and worried, imagining them being sucked out with every jerky movement of the machine.

'The range of the helicopter is limited. We've been here long enough. Home, James.' Duncan nodded to the pilot who gave him the thumbs up sign and wheeled the whirlybird away towards Aberdeen, the three survivors huddled close together in survival bags to conserve body heat.

Andrea could have done with some of Duncan's body heat too by the time they reached the hospital with their patients. Despite all the clothing, she was frozen, especially her feet. He did not stop monitoring the men's condition till each of the survivors was safely in the dry, warm environment of intensive care beds, slowly rewarming and recovering.

'And now you'll need a hot bath and a hot drink,' he said, being careful not to smile at her dishevelled appearance. She had oil smeared on her cheek and her thick hair hung in rats' tails. 'And that's an order.'

'A Hunter's special?'

'Exactly. Before those pretty teeth start chattering,' he grinned. 'You did well, Andrea. I'm glad you came along. I couldn't have managed on my own.'

The words washed over her as warming as a glass of Glenhunter and Andrea turned away so that he would not see her smile of pleasure. Did that mean he had accepted her? That he agreed that she could cope perfectly well on the rig? She had to ask him. She could not stop herself.

'Does that mean that I've passed the test as a rig medic too? That at last you've given up trying to get my contract cancelled?'

It was a mistake. She knew immediately she had said the wrong thing as his darkened face clouded over and set in stern lines.

'Dammit, woman. You know I don't approve and never will. Your presence is likely to jeopardise the safety of the entire crew because you are a woman. Rig work is man's work. You couldn't cope if there was a major disaster, especially a woman like you, living on your nerves. A woman's place is in. . .on shore, not on a floating time-bomb.'

'You nearly said "in the home", Doctor, didn't you?' Andrea's voice was distorted with anger. 'What quaint old-fashioned ideas you have. Haven't you heard of emancipation and equal opportunties? It's all the rage down south.'

'I'm talking about here and now, and you can have every equal opportunity you want — on shore. It's time you came to your senses, Andrea. I want you safe and in one piece, because I care about you. God knows why, but I do.'

Andrea froze in her boots, the sounds of the busy hospital washing round her like acoustic wallpaper.

A small voice told her she would lose him if she persisted.

'Thank you for that overwhelming vote of confidence in my ability,' she said. The colour seemed to drain away from everything. 'I presume you'll be giving me an outstanding reference.'

'If that's what you want.'

No, it wasn't what Andrea wanted. But she couldn't tell Duncan that she was falling in love with him. She did not want to fall in love with anyone, ever again.

CHAPTER SEVEN

'YOU'LL be wanting to get home and out of those wet clothes. I have a dinner engagement,' Duncan said in a businesslike manner. 'I'll call you a taxi.'

A dinner engagement. . .it produced a kind of ache from the impossibility of accepting that Duncan might already have a woman in his life. Of course, she must be the occupant of the peach and white bedroom. She had turned up again. Andrea felt crushed between the past and the future. But why shouldn't he? The most eligible bachelor for miles would hardly live like a monk.

'Don't bother,' she said. 'I can see myself home.'

She must get away. Anywhere. So that she could pull herself together into some sort of workable shape.

An ambulance driver trod on his brakes. Andrea's face went white. She had been stumbling across the forecourt of the hospital without looking. She sent the driver a stricken look of apology and tried to gather her scattered wits.

'Are you all right?' he asked out of the window.

'Sorry, my fault. I think my brain got frostbite in that helicopter.'

131

'Can I give you a lift, Sister? I'm going south of the city to a call from an old people's home.'

'Is it anywhere near Hunter's Lodge, Dr Hunter's place?'

'Hop in, Sister. I can drop you right at the end of the road.'

The driver and his colleague made room for her, but they could see she was grey-faced and worn out and did not pump her for details of the rescue. The story had gone round the hospital grapevine fast enough. She thanked them wearily when, some rumbling miles later, the driver slowed down to stop and she recognised the road. Her footsteps quickened with the thought of a hot bath and clean clothes and something warm inside her.

The flat in the coachhouse was suddenly home and welcoming. Even the cobwebs in the vaulted ceiling were familiar. She turned on the lights and the electric fire and the radio for some music, shedding clothes as she went to the bathroom, stepping out of them carelessly. She turned on both taps and poured in scented magnolia foam with abandon. She wanted steam to the ceiling, foam to her eyebrows and a whole evening to herself.

She drew all the curtains. The gathering night reflected her melancholy and she wanted to shut it out. First Lucas and now Duncan. She was a fool of the first order. Hadn't she learned her lesson from her affair with Lucas? For the first time she admitted to herself that it had been an affair. She had been besotted with him, living for those stolen moments together, believing his lies. Even when she had discovered he was married and intended to stay married, she still could not keep away.

But she had had some pride. Her reluctance to make love had angered him. Then one day she had seen him in his car with his wife and she'd looked so nice. In the back of the car, safely strapped in, were two small children. That, then, was the end.

Her eyes filled with tears for the hurt person she had been. But her tears dried as it dawned on her that Lucas had become a shadowy figure in her mind, and she remembered his handsomeness now as a slightly unsavoury whole but not each perfect feature. She was quite over him. It was like a burden slipping from her shoulders. It was Duncan who filled her thoughts and dreams. Her feelings for the tall Scots doctor were running dangerously deep.

She soaked so long in the bath that the water cooled round her, the tips of her fingers wrinkled, and the foam bubbles popped and vanished. She climbed out, rubbing her skin lethargically, and wrapped herself in a cotton robe, knotting the tie around her waist. The long sitting-room was warming up and she curled on the settee, knees tucked up, letting the weariness eddy in waves. What a day. . .in many ways quite wonderful: time alone with Duncan, working with him, rescuing those young fishermen together. Heavy wet hair fell over her face and she brushed it back with her fingers, not caring if it dried in a tangle. She was on leave. It didn't matter what she looked like.

The music was soothing and melodic, her frayed nerves lapping up the rhythmic softness and blurred chords. She dozed off and never heard the footsteps coming up the stairs. Nor had she bothered to lock the door and the man came in without hindrance.

'Don't you ever bolt your door?' said Duncan, walking in. 'It's pretty dangerous.'

Andrea shot up, awake in a instant, the robe falling open at the neck, rosy skin on view and the rising curves of her breasts like gentle hills. She covered herself quickly, colour flooding her cheeks.

'That's the second time. Don't you ever knock?'

'I was worried about you. I wasn't sure if you had got home all right. I ordered a taxi but you'd gone. The lights were on up here and the radio blaring but that didn't mean anything. You could have drowned in your bath.'

'Don't be silly,' said Andrea, sliding her slim legs off the sofa and going to turn off the radio, which had changed programme while she slept.

Brass bands were not her style. 'Why should I drown?'

'Epileptic fit.'

'I appreciate your concern but you know from my medical file that I haven't got epilepsy.' Suddenly she realised the lateness. 'Aren't you supposed to be out dining? Some engagement?'

'I cancelled,' said Duncan, his voice giving away nothing. Then, seeing the expression on her face, he added, 'It was a civic thing. Very boring.'

'You don't have to explain anything,' said Andrea tartly. She marched into the minuscule kitchen and put on the kettle, making a lot of unnecessary noise. She was working herself up into a terrible temper just on supposition. 'It's obvious that you must have a personal life here in Aberdeen.'

'I don't know why you're so offended and upset. I've lived here all my life apart from my service in the navy. I love Aberdeen. It's my home. My roots are here.'

'And your home has a nice little love-nest. All ready and waiting for each new occupant.'

'What a waspish tongue you have at times, Sister West. I pity any man you get your claws into.'

'Wasps don't have claws. But they do have a lethal sting and I wouldn't hesitate to use it on any man who was annoying me.' But she hadn't, she hadn't. She had simply crawled away from

Lucas, licking her wounds, hiding from the world. 'Don't worry. You're quite safe. I won't ever occupy your peachy love-nest. Tea or coffee?'

'Tea please. With a wee dram.' He produced a bottle of Glenhunter from behind his back. It was then she realised he had not changed. He was still in the same clothes, now dried on him, wrinkled and creased like a scarecrow. Something must have happened at the hospital and he had been called to stay and assist.

'You haven't changed and you haven't gone out. What's happened?'

'One of the young men we rescued collapsed suddenly. . .all the signs of torpor, muscle rigidity, dilated pupils. We thought we'd lost him. But we got him breathing again.'

Andrea caught her breath and shook her head. She could imagine the scene, the rush of the emergency team. The EKG machine, the defibrillator paddles jerking his heart back to life, getting the young man to breath again. 'Funny how even conscious survivors can collapse and become unconscious after rescue. It only underlines that they should never be left alone.'

'Is that a gentle hint that I ought to be more grateful that you came along with me?'

'Not a gentle hint. More of a thumping big reminder.'

Duncan smiled and it transformed his stern face. Her anger died like a blown flame. Andrea tried to concentrate on making the tea and forgetting the tall man so near her in the confines of the small kitchen. She was also very aware of her near nakedness and the hot perfume of her skin. The bright cotton robe was well wrapped round her waist but they both knew she had nothing on underneath.

His fingers were on the back of her neck, among the glossy wet hair, kneading the muscles with firm but gentle fingers. She felt herself leaning against him, the unexpected massage soothing her nerves.

'You're very tense,' he murmured.

'Tired,' she said.

She was so deliciously aware of his fingers kneading her skin that all her caution and distress disappeared. He only had to touch her and the voice of her body told her she was lost.

He turned her round and kissed her, a sweet, undemanding kiss that took her by surprise. She did not respond but drank in the feel of his mouth, storing the memory, letting it take away some of her pain and hurt. She did not want to be hurt again. She did not want to be taken in by a man and used. Yet she had to admit that this kiss was different. She needed Duncan and wanted him with every breath of her body. If he swept her off to that patchwork bed on the raised platform, she would not resist him.

Instead he locked his arms round her waist and

leaned back, regarding her with a quizzical look. The shadows etched under his eyes were a reminder of his recent illness; the man had clearly overdone it today.

'Isn't this somewhat dangerous?' he mocked.

'Very,' she said. 'I have very little on and your woman friend is probably armed with some sort of geologist's axe.'

'Passion is often dangerous as well as wonderful.'

'Then I vote for staying on the safe side,' she said but she did not mean one word. She could not trust herself when she was near him.

'Too much safety isn't living,' he said deeply. 'You're a lovely woman, Andrea, when you're not glaring at me and making a stand for your rights. Look at this skin. . .' He brushed her dewy cheek with the tip of his fingers. 'Like silk. . .it's beautiful.'

No one had ever told her she was beautiful before. She glowed and blossomed, began to shine. It was extraordinary. Yet she felt she was being examined under a microscope; knew she had not properly cleaned off her make-up. She probably had panda-eyes from smudged mascara.

'What axe and what's all this about a love-nest?' he went on, his eyes glinting. 'You don't mean Morag's room? She's my baby sister, an air hostess on long-haul flights. She just calls in to wash her hair.'

'Your sister's room? Her clothes and make-up?'

He nodded. 'But you're quite right, I've met someone, someone very special, a woman a hundred times more intelligent and innocently beautiful than my scatterbrained sister.'

Andrea felt she had been hit by a rock right in the middle of her solar plexus. She forgot how to breathe and had to draw in air fast. Of course Duncan would have found someone.

Aberdeen was a cosmopolitan city, the Flower of Scotland, full of elegant, well-dressed woman in good jobs making their contribution to its concerts, theatres, the university life. How could he not have met a woman who matched him for intelligence, energy, care and diligence. He often looked so sinewy, laconic, and watchful, remote and on guard, yet Duncan needed and deserved a warm-blooded woman to bring out all that deserved love and passion and who would love him wholeheartedly in return.

'I'm glad,' said Andrea, unfastening his fingers from round her waist. 'Everyone needs someone. Now how about that tea? It's getting cold.'

'What should I do without you to look after me?' He took the mug of tea and added an inch of whisky like a born Scot. He settled himself in a corner of the sofa as if he lived there, which he had once long ago, staring into the flickering glow of the fire as he sipped the fiery brew. Andrea wondered what he was thinking about. . .that special woman, of course. She rescued the mug from his hands as he nodded off.

She slipped off Duncan's shoes. This was getting to be a habit. Then she covered him with a tartan rug from a cupboard. He was dead to the world. She took herself off to bed with a book but had read no more than a page before her eyes became impossible to keep open and she only just had time to switch off the lamp.

'It's like painting the Forth Bridge,' the man mumbled, biting his swollen lip against the pain. He was one of Lochinvar's team of six permanent painters. 'It's the wind, y'know, scouring the surface of the steel night and day. A coat of paint only lasts five years out here.'

The painter had slipped on the pipe deck. He had facial cuts, two black eyes and lost a tooth. He tried a gappy grin. 'Shall I live, Sister?'

'You'll be back at gritblasting in no time at all. But I'll make an appointment for you to see the dentist onshore. Can't have that devastating Brummy smile at half-mast. And you ought to see Dr Hunter at the same time. I'm sure there's no damage to the retina or bleeding into the eyeball, but I'd like him to confirm it.'

Andrea pushed away the overhead lamp that she had been using to make the eye examination. There were so many eye injuries in this work that she had quite got over her squeamishness in making the examination.

She put cold compresses on his eyes, cleaned up the cuts, gave him the standard antibiotic injection.

'Wot, no raw steaks?'

'Only on the supper menu, Reg.'

She had only been back on the rig three days and already her two weeks flat-hunting onshore were a confused memory. Andrea had been determined to find her own flat but there was nothing available in her price range. She had stayed on at the coachhouse, wishing she did not like it so much.

Tom Groves, the camp boss, had saved her cabin for her and she had brought back some water-colours of the River Don to hang on the walls. And she now had fine bone-china floral cups and saucers for her tea and coffee. It looked pretty on the tray and she had replaced the plastic spoons with some old silver ones she had found in an antique shop in a cobbled street.

But Duncan was not a dim memory. He was firmly entrenched in her heart. Every expression, every word, every kiss. It hurt that she was too late and that he had already met a special woman. She had to remind herself that she had only been around five minutes, was here to work and save enough money to help pay off her father's debts.

Romance did not appear anywhere on her list of priorities.

'Are you sure you're all right?' her mother said on the phone. 'You sound a bit quiet, love.'

'It's just a bad line, Mum.'

'Are you sleeping all right?'

'Well, the noise is pretty awful. It takes a lot of getting used to. They put sound-proofing in the sleeping quarters but the noise level is still high.'

'Can't they shut it off at night?'

Andrea had to laugh. 'No, Mum. . .a rig works twenty-four hours non-stop.'

The usual procession of coughs, colds and skin complaints arrived at Andrea's surgery that morning. She heard the helicopter landing on the helideck and hoped it did not herald the arrival of Duncan. She had not seen him since that night when he had fallen asleep on her sofa. When she awoke the next morning, he had gone.

Andrea slammed some instruments into the steriliser, her fingers tapping on the lid. A man was being brought into the surgery, a driller by the look of his blood-stained clothes.

Andrea turned her attention to the injured man. 'Hello,' she said cheerfully. 'What's your name? Haven't I seen you before?'

'Yes, Sister Mae. Dandruff Dan. But it's a bit more serious this time. Got a nasty cut.'

She was able to clean him up, sort him out with

antibiotics, send him back to the cafeteria with a few stitches and his arm in a sling.

Andrea closed her eyes in relief and leaned against the wall, trying to draw strength from some inner source of steel. She wanted to see Duncan desperately, to hear from his own mouth about this other woman in his life. Had he only been saying that so that she would calm down? She wanted to know for sure so that she could stamp out her yearning with cold common sense and get on with living in the real world. She was not being kind to herself with all this self-torture.

'What self-torture, Sister?' said Duncan, strolling into the surgery. 'Been practising suturing on yourself?'

Andrea had not realised she'd spoken out aloud. Duncan stood, rocking on his heels, hands in his pockets. 'I was rehearsing my safety lecture for this evening,' she improvised quickly.

He raised a dark eye-brow but did not pursue the point. 'Are you any good at splinters?'

'It depends where they are,' she said demurely. His sudden appearance was filling her with a silent delight. She did not think about the special woman in his life. Just having him to herself and talking to her was enough for the moment. She would settle for that.

'Nowhere embarrassing, I assure you, but pretty messy. I can't get it out myself. It's a steel splinter.'

The fragment was embedded under his thumb nail. It had become infected and was red and swollen.

'Funny how doctors neglect themselves,' she said, preparing a bowl of cetrimide one per cent solution for cleansing the surrounding skin and wound if necessary. 'How long have you had this? You should have taken it out before it got infected.'

'Didn't have time,' he said.

Andrea plucked out the splinter carefully. She held a piece of dressing over the weeping wound to staunch the bleeding, staring at the ceiling, looking anywhere but at him. The atmosphere was taut.

'This is my second hitch,' she said. 'Can you tell me if my job is still under the chopper?'

'The apppointment is being reviewed. Apparently, as it was an emergency, they felt they couldn't wait until my return. I am to monitor your work and put in a report.'

'That's wonderful. You of all people and you can hardly say you're unbiased. What else will you take into consideration: performance in bed?'

His jaw set, eyes cold and blank. 'I'll pretend you didn't say that. I'll try to forget how soft and pliant you were in my arms. Be honest, Andrea, you wanted it as much as I did. You might lie to me, but your body doesn't lie.'

Andrea was taken aback by the vehemence of his defence. She tried to find the right words.

'It was a mistake,' she said weakly. This was getting seriously out of hand. She had not meant to antagonise him, only get to the truth.

His eyes were blazing, his voice dangerously low. Andrea stiffened. His anger was draining her will power. She tried to quieten her ragged breathing, to drag her thoughts into some coherence.

'No, of course, that's not what I meant,' she began.

'Then what did you mean?'

She could not bring herself to speak. She could hardly remember what she had been going to say. 'I don't know what I mean. . .'

'You want to pull yourself together,' he said more kindly but letting go of her abruptly. 'I know rig work can get to people. They become depressed, fantasise, get hooked on tranquillisers.' He shot a meaningful look at her locked drugs cabinet. 'It could happen to anyone. After all, you are basically a shore nurse and the isolation is a strain. Perhaps you ought to have a word with the company psychiatrist.'

Duncan took no notice of her gasp. He looked detached. 'You told me you hadn't been sleeping well. I've found you crying a couple of times. And you are always thirsty—a common minor side effect of amitriptyline is dryness of the mouth.'

'For heaven's sake, don't be so ridiculous,' said

Andrea, snapping into a cool, professional voice. 'Since when has being occasionally thirsty been a symptom of depression? People are often thirsty. I like tea. I like coffee. That doesn't mean I'm on tranquillisers. You may have noticed the temperature inside the rig is fairly warm despite the cold weather outside. As for crying, I have just got over an emotional upheaval and the death of my father. Like a lot of women, having the odd cry does help. It also happens to be damned noisy on the rig and I'm not the only one having trouble sleeping. You want to try it yourself.' She mentally tightened her belt a notch. 'And while I'm at it, Dr Hunter, telling a patient to pull themselves together is hardly the correct way to go about treating an undiagnosed depressive.'

'Emotional upheaval? You mean some man?'

'Of course. Dozens of them. All the time.'

They stared at each other in shock. Neither had ever been so angry before. The expression in his eyes was unreadable. He was mad with untrammelled passion. Despite the warmth of the surgery, Andrea felt chilled to the bone. What had she done? She wanted to pull him to her, tell him she'd been talking nonsense, to cleave herself to him, claim him, cover his face with maddening kisses.

'Thank you for making your feelings so clear,' said Duncan coldly, his voice twisted with menace. 'I thought I knew you, but I obviously don't. I'll keep out of your way, except in a professional capacity.'

Then he was gone, leaving only the impression of his height, the power, the strength of his dark, worn face.

Andrea heard a low moan. She did not know it came from her own throat.

CHAPTER EIGHT

DUNCAN kept his word. She hardly saw him over the next few hitches and though she stayed at the coachhouse when she was on leave, it was only the XJ6 that she ever saw or heard, purring in or out like a sleek tiger.

If in doubt, radio for medical advice. The words were a litany for Andrea and every day she repeated them to herself. There were times when she had to radio for Duncan's advice though often she got one of the other doctors on call.

When she did speak to him, there was an edge of irritation in his voice. 'Can't you deal with this yourself, Sister West? I'm just going out on another call.'

'Of course I can. But fractures to the elbow are very dangerous, as you well know. The injury needs to be X-rayed at hospital.'

'I'll send someone out to the rig to bring him back. What's his name?'

'Eric Parsons. He's a crane driver.'

'Thank you, sister. I've noted his name.'

She went back to the injured man, hurt by Duncan's indifference to her. It was something she could not get used to. She tried to put the tone of his voice behind her and concentrate on her patient. 'You'll soon be on top of the world again,' she said.

'Height's not the problem' he croaked, nursing his broken elbow. 'But working a crane on a rig is very different from a shore job. The wind's getting up, over forty knots. The load was swinging all over the place. I was constantly having to adjust.'

'Funny how fast the weather can change. It was sunny this morning, a lovely clear sky, and look at it now,' said Andrea, remembering the grey-laced sea as she had climbed a catwalk for a breath of air and to take food to her birds. 'I'm going to have to straighten your arm and it may hurt. Yell out if you want to. Let's get you up on the couch. I'll try to be quick.'

She wondered if she was going to be able to do it. She knew the theory, but putting it into practice was difficult. There was no point in telling Eric that she had never done it on her own before.

She monitored the area of the fracture carefully, looking for damage to blood vessels and nerves around the elbow. She checked the driver's fingertips for blueness or whiteness, any lack of feeling or altered feeling, wishing Duncan were with her to confirm her findings. Slowly she brought the arm and forearm forward and steadily to the man's side, applying gentle traction to stop the limb shortening.

Sweat broke out on his grimy forehead, but Eric was built like an ox and made of stern stuff.

'That's it,' she said. 'All over. You didn't want your pint arm an inch shorter, did you?'

Andrea put plenty of loose padding between the arm and the body, and around the injured joint. Then she encircled both his body and arm with bandages, binding the forearm to his trunk, checking that the ties were firm but not too tight and restricting circulation.

'I feel like a trussed turkey,' he grinned. 'All this for a broken elbow.'

'It's important to immobilise the limb,' said Andrea. 'We've got to make you as comfortable as possible for the flight.'

She prepared a pain-killing injection. Eric might refuse it. He was one of those tough nuts.

'I shall miss your lecture tonight, Sister.'

Her lectures on safety and hygiene were being well received and already there was a slight decrease in minor eye and face injuries as the workforce remembered to wear goggles and masks. She had also organised several bridge evenings which had been popular even when the bidding became competitive and intense. The Scrabble evening had been less successful because of a tendency to cheat on the spelling of words. The talent contest had been a riot and an evening best forgotten, though the men thought it was great.

Andrea was making friends among the staff but was careful to keep her distance from the men in case her smallest smile or pleasantry should be misinterpreted. The rig was a floating village and it was all too easy for friendships to spring up and develop into relationships which on shore would never have even got started.

She wrote long reassuring letters to her mother, making light of the extreme weather conditions and concentrating on the satisfying work.

'My cabin is looking really nice now,' she wrote in her long sloping writing. 'I've hung some water-colours on the walls. One of the cooks has given me some cuttings from her plants and I'm trying to grow them in tea leaves. I must remember to bring some earth back next time I'm on shore.'

The rain was travelling sideways, waves splashing upwards like a waterfall gone berserk. Droves of birds dashed themselves on to the platform for shelter only to be swept off by the next gust. Andrea struggled outside to accompany Eric to the helicopter, her waterproofs slashed with rain in seconds, flattened against her body by the wind. The stretcher carriers battled each step along the gangways.

'It's getting worse,' one of them shouted to her. She nodded back, not wasting her breath, wondering if the flight would be cancelled.

The helicopter was hovering on the helideck, blades still rotating at slow speed, waiting impatiently to launch off into the last limpid hour of daylight. The pilot could not close down the chopper's engines because the rotor might sail under the wind strain and take the aircraft's tail off.

'Must be forty-five knots at least,' someone else yelled. 'The rough weather's building up. Doubt if the chopper'll get out to us again till this lot settles.'

Andrea's spine tingled with fear. The catwalks were slippery and dangerous. It was like walking a tightrope with no safety net. The pilots were so brave and skilled and Duncan was out there somewhere on a call, relying on the pilot to bring him back. As she hung on to a handrail, she prayed that the helicopters would take off without mishap and fly her patient and his patient to shore and shelter.

She could not breathe freely until the chopper was a dark insect winging skywards. Only then did she turn and struggle down the maze of gangways and platforms to the living quarters below, her face dripping with rain. Where were all her sea-birds now? She hoped they had found shelter under the platform itself. There were plenty of nooks and crannies in the vast structure to cling on to.

Boots and hard hat and waterproofs were shed in an area called the dusty bin. Tom Groves was strict about keeping the living quarters clean and dry. Outside everything was very dirty, particularly the drill floor, and he was determined that every corner of accommodation should stay clean so that the men had a break from their working conditions.

Andrea felt she deserved a quick coffee and one of the chef's delicious French pastries. She joined a group of production mechanics whose job was to operate the plant. They were also responsible for the platform's mechanical equipment and spare parts.

'The weather must have reached the safety limit for cranes. Eric was unlucky,' she said, sitting down.

'I wouldn't be surprised if the on-shore gas terminal tell us to cut a few million off,' said one of the mechanics, putting mustard on a thick ham sandwich.

'Your turn to adjust the control valve,' joked another. 'Then you can do the blocked loo on level three.'

'Don't like the sound of that weather. Wind's changing. I think I'll take a set of readings and check everything's running OK.'

Andrea could hear that the weather was worsening. The sky outside was the colour of dark slate. She knew the big platform was structurally sound but it was a semi-submersible, a floater, with its hulls only submerged in the sea and not resting firmly on the seabed. They had a reputation for stability in the wild, deep water of the North Sea. But Andrea was not one hundred per cent convinced as the rain slashed at the windows and the wind howled. Lochinvar felt as vulnerable as any ship afloat.

The dining-room door flew open, caught in a cross current of air from the outer door being opened. The turbulence scattered paper napkins and blew curtains apart. It was like a chill hand clutching the room and shaking it.

The men who came in were drenched and looking pretty shattered. They went straight to the coffee counter. One of them was Duncan, his thick hair plastered to his head. He came over to her table, his hands clamped round the hot mug. Her heart leaped at the sight of him.

'Hello, Andrea. We had to put down on Lochinvar,' he said as if accounting for his presence. He wiped at his face. 'It was an emergency landing. Some obstruction in the engine, probably a bird.'

Andrea flinched but she did not know if it was for bird or men. She was concerned for all of them.

'I've a patient from another rig. They are bringing him down now. Can we put him in your sick-bay? It's a crush injury. A driller. Very nasty.'

He was still standing, itching to go back to his patient after a few reviving mouthfuls of coffee.

But he had come to ask her permission first, everything by the book; it was his way.

'Yes, of course,' she said, finishing her coffee in a gulp. It was obvious they would all have to stay overnight or at least until the weather improved.

This was work. Andrea was happy to have Duncan around for a few hours, perhaps get a chance to talk to him, 'I'll come right away. I just hope my elbow fracture has reached Aberdeen all right.'

'Jeff could check by radio for you. It would put your mind at rest.'

The rig was going to be crowded that night. A shift that was due to leave, couldn't go. Tom was busy trying to find extra accommodation; people were having to double up. The wind-lashed, wave-lashed structure shuddered under the force. For the first time Andrea felt a real shaft of fear, the taste of ash in her mouth.

'I mean, Lochinvar is very strong, isn't it?' she asked vaguely as they hurried to the sick bay. It felt about as secure as a cardboard doll's house.

'Solid as a rock,' he said, keeping the concern out of his voice. At this rate the rig would have to shut down production. And he knew from experience that there would be more than the usual number of casualties as the giant platform was made secure. As they swung into the sick bay, he peered at Andrea's face, noting the faint blue shadows on her wan face. She was still not sleeping well.

'Not scared, are you?'

'Of course not.'

He wanted to say that he was here; he would look after her but he couldn't get the right words out. 'Nothing to be scared about,' he grunted, annoyed at his failure. 'Just a bit windy.'

'I know. Was the flight rough?'

He nodded. 'I don't know how the pilot kept control. The cross winds were buffeting the aircraft from all directions. It was very unstable. They call it wind shear. I don't think we would have made it to Aberdeen. That seagull did us a favour.'

'Sacrificed in the line of duty,' said Andrea, trying to sound light-hearted, but all she could think of was that Duncan might have been ditched in that storm-tossed sea, struggling for survivial in temperatures below freezing, his first thought being to keep his patient afloat.

'What happened?' she asked, reorganising her sickbay to accommodate the injured man.

'There was a freak accident. A floorhand was using air tongs to spin out rather than rotate out, and the air tongs had been placed on a stand to spin the pipe apart.'

Andrea looked blank. She had learned a lot about oil production while living on Lochinvar but this was new to her.

'They were unscrewing a pipe?'

'Right. The driller tried to find out if the stand was free but the stand suddenly jumped free from the bottom pipe. The floorhand hadn't time to release the tongs and he got caught between the snubline and the tongs.'

Andrea closed her eyes in horror. 'How awful. Poor man. . .?'

'Unfortunately, no. The floorhand broke his neck. It's the driller I'm bringing in. The pipe swung back on his leg. There's considerable damage to the muscles and other soft tissues. He's in severe shock. We shall have to watch him. There may be internal bleeding.'

Andrea would have to monitor his temperature and pulse rate throughout the night at half-hourly intervals. Goodbye, sleep, she thought. Soft tissue bleeding would lead to bruising but the formation of more blood in the deeper tissues could cause painful swelling.

The driller was pallid, shivering, his lips and edges of the ears were blue even though he had been warmly wrapped for the journey. His pulse was rapid and weak. They laid him on a bed, covered him, raising the end so that his feet and legs were elevated. Duncan had already immobolised the crushed leg and supported it in the most comfortable position. He had also fixed up a saline drip. Andrea gave the sighing man sips of water.

'You'll be all right now,' said Andrea encouragingly. 'We'll give you something to ease the pain.'

'Glad to be off that whirlybird, Doc,' he mumbled restlessly, arms twitching. 'I was. . . starting to feel really. . .sick.'

Andrea prepared a standard dose of fifteen milligrams of morphine. It was important to reduce the man's restlessness and it would help him if he slept through the storm.

'We'll do two-hour shifts each,' said Duncan, surprising her. 'If we get any chance at all. A storm like this usually produces a lot of minor casualties. We're in for a busy night. You'd better go first. I'll wake you if I need help.'

'Thanks,' said Andrea. 'That's really nice of you. Even two hours would be a blessing.'

'And you'll need another jersey when they close down the production. The heat will drop. You'll feel the difference.'

Andrea moved out of the proud and shadowy shelter that enclosed her and let him see her smile. 'Why are you being nice to me?'

'Don't know,' he said, pretending to scratch his head. 'And I haven't uttered a single word of criticism. Is that called progress?'

'Indeed,' she agreed. 'I hardly know what I've done to deserve it. Perhaps it's the storm. You're disorientated by the strong winds.'

'That may be the reason, or perhaps I've simply

missed you. Funny thing, missing a person. It's like a gap in one's life that ought to be filled.'

Andrea suddenly lost track of what she was doing. The room went out of focus. She clenched her fingers into fists at her side. Now she was glimpsing the Duncan that always enchanted her, tall, charming, funny, capricious.

'It must be a ploy, softening me up. You obviously want something,' said Andrea, hiding her pleasure.

'I want to share your bed,' he said, taking her aside, well out of hearing of their patient. It was surprising what sharp ears even unconscious patients had. 'But don't be alarmed, Andrea. I suggested a two-hour shift and never the twain shall meet.'

'I should be delighted to share my bed with you,' Andrea murmured, 'I'll warm it up for you.'

'I hoped you'd say that.'

Pete Overton hovered in the doorway and cleared his throat. 'Sorry to interrupt. There's a bit of a problem in accommodation. . .but it's your department, Sister.'

Andrea hurried over. She knew that Pete would not have come down if it was not really necessary. He was one of the men on the rig who kept severely out of her way though she had no idea why. 'What is it?'

'One of the men has locked himself in his cabin. He shares with three other men. We know he's been feeling a bit low, a bit down, since his ulcer but we thought he'd really picked up physically since he got back.'

'Have there been any similar episodes?'

'Yes, a week ago. He was very irritable all day then again wouldn't come out of his cabin. Morose and sullen. The other medic talked him out, hours later, gave him something. Mike's always been a bit volatile, but it seems to have got worse lately.'

'Is this the same Mike who had a bleeding peptic ulceration back in the late summer?' Duncan asked.

'The same,' Pete nodded. 'He's been behaving very strangely. Bizarre, actually. First of all, making complaints about his bed—said someone had nicked his mattress—then the shaving mirror got shattered because he didn't like the face in it. Then it was the air-conditioning. He said he could hear a knocking in the pipes and someone was trying to get in. We investigated it but couldn't find a thing.'

'Sister?' Duncan looked at her enquiringly.

'Yes, I know Mike. He was prescribed a very small amount of valium by the last medic. Mike apparently has domestic problems at home and was feeling anxious. A girlfriend I think. Or perhaps it's several girlfriends.'

'Sounds like something for the experts. All we can do here is handle the situation sympathetically and see if he needs more skilled help on shore. It might seem odd to us but everything is probably very real to him,' said Duncan. 'He really thinks someone has taken his mattress or is trying to get into his room.'

Andrea knew that the isolation of rig work from homes and families often got to people and caused mental problems, anxiety and depression. But very depressed people could commit suicide and it was essential to discover quickly if there was any kind of risk with Mike. If she kept very calm and friendly and sympathetic she might be able to find out just how ill he was.

'Would you like me to come with you?'

'Yes please, Dr Hunter. That would be very helpful.' It was always wise to have two people present if a man's behaviour was unpredictable. 'I think I'll need you.'

Duncan opened his mouth to say something but then changed his mind. It was the first time that Andrea had admitted that she might need him. The words were sweet indeed.

'I'll get someone to keep an eye on your patient here while you're gone,' said Pete, striding off.

It was up a floor to the four-berth cabins. They were cramped quarters with bunk beds and little privacy for each man. Outside a couple of men in check workshirts and jeans were lounging against the walls, talking in low voices.

'Can you get the so-and-so to unlock the door, Sister? We want to get in to get our things.'

'Gone off his rocker, Sister.'

'What has Mike been saying?'

'Oh, things about not wanting to live and stuff like that. Calling out. . .and bits of rubbish. It's been going on for ages.'

'Why didn't someone come for me sooner?'

'We thought he'd been drinking.'

'And has he?' Alcohol was strictly forbidden on the rig but some men were devious at smuggling in a bottle.

'Dunno.'

Andrea went close to the cabin door and knocked politely. She could hear nothing. 'Mike? Hello, Mike. It's Sister West here. Can I talk to you?'

They heard a scrabbling about and the scraping of furniture being moved. 'That's a locker,' said one of the men. 'He's put it in front of the door.'

'Mike, listen to me. I only want to talk to you. Will you open the door and let me come in?'

There was an ominous silence. Then suddenly Mike shouted ferociously in a wild voice, 'Go away! *Go away. It's too late. Get this man away.*'

Andrea's hopes for an easy solution disappeared. A severely disturbed patient was the last thing they wanted on a night like this. It might even be the weather that had finally cracked Mike. Weather was a funny thing with some people. Wind set people's teeth on edge; a coming thunderstorm gave them a headache; the moon drove people to suicide and murder.

'I think you need someone to talk to,' Andrea went on in a friendly voice. 'So I won't go away yet. Are you feeling tired? I could give you something to help you sleep, Mike.'

Duncan gave her a silent thumbs-up sign.

'Would you like that, Mike? Something to help you get to sleep. Perhaps you'd like a cup of tea as well. We'll get one for you.' She nodded and one of the men hurried away to the cafeteria, glad to have an errand to do in a normal environment.

'There's someone trying to get into my room,' Mike moaned. They heard sniffing as if he was crying too. 'It's Jim. He's behind the wall. I know it's that bastard Jim. He said he'd get me.'

'He'd have to swim a long way to get here,' said Andrea without thinking, but the words were out before she could stop them.

'He's got a boat, damn you!' Mike howled, beating the locker door.

Andrea knew that had been a thoughtless remark. It didn't help to contradict or argue or joke, however irrational Mike might be.

'Shall I come in and look around for Jim?' she said quickly. 'Then I can tell him to go away.' She went on talking to Mike in this way for several minutes, trying to sound understanding and sympathetic. They heard a lot of jerky, then ripping noises.

'Whatever's going on?' someone whispered.

'Would you please open the door and let me come in,' Andrea tried again.

'No, you can't,' Mike yelled. 'No one can help me. It's all over. I can't go on. . .I can't go on. . .'

Andrea looked helplessly at Duncan. She was not doing very well. 'Do we know who Jim is?' she asked his mate, moving back from the door.

'He's the husband of one of Mike's girlfriends, we think. Or it could be it's his wife's new boyfriend, we're not sure. Mike lives a complicated life. Don't know how he does it. Reckon he comes on the rig for a bit of peace and quiet.'

Oh, dear, thought Andrea. She did not want to know. It sounded like the tangle that was all too common these days. Everything got so involved and some people were just not emotionally equipped to cope. She had not been able to cope and she bitterly regretted all that lost time and wasted emotion. She had been crippled by disappointment. But now she was beginning to learn to live and breathe freely again.

'Sister West? Sister West.' Duncan's voice interrupted her thoughts. 'I don't like what I'm not hearing,' he said. 'I think it's time to get the master key from Tom Groves and go on in. Have you a twenty-five milligram chlorpromazine, intramuscular injection in the drugs cabinet? He may be violent. Best to be prepared.'

Andrea nodded. 'OK. I'll bring fifty milligrams

of amitriptyline as well. If he calms down. . .an anti-depressive will be sufficient.'

'He'll need to be in a cabin on his own and should be confined to that cabin. Can we arrange that? The rig is no place for anyone thinking of throwing themselves over the side, especially in a storm. All sharp things, razors, knives, mirrors, bottles, string and rope must be removed.'

'Tom will sort all that out. I'll make sure,' said Andrea. 'But it won't be easy. He's very short of space tonight.'

'We'll move out,' offered Mike's other cabin mate. 'No problem. We'll doss down somewhere else. There's sofas in the lounge. . .if we don't suffocate on the cigarette smoke.'

'Thank you,' said Andrea, with a big smile. 'That's really helpful.'

'I'll fetch Tom Groves, too.'

'Good, at the double. I'll talk to Mike some more. That sounds as if he's tearing up sheets.'

Andrea ran all the way. In minutes she was back with the medication, Tom Groves arrived with the key, the other cabin mate with a tray of tea and a bemused expression at the drama that was unfolding.

'Armed to the teeth,' she declared, a little unsteadily, catching her breath. There was no knowing what they would find.

Duncan shot her an approving, comforting

look, his dark eyes holding hers with the look, giving her courage, sharing the wealth of his experience. 'Ready to go in, Sister?'

'Ready when you are.'

CHAPTER NINE

ANDREA felt sure that the rig was beginning to sway. It was an unnerving feeling. She did not mention her wobbly knees to Duncan as they spoke only briefly while Mike was calmed and sedated.

They had reached him only just in time. He had been tearing up sheets and knotting them together to make a rope. Its purpose was not clear. Now he was sleeping peacefully. He had the room to himself and his pals were taking turns to sit with him in case he woke in any distress.

The storm was increasing in intensity. Jeff Knightly, the radio operator, had passed on the forecast from the meteorological office and all rig personnel were warned to stay inside as freak waves were in the vicinity.

The rig production closed down and the uncanny silence made the storm sounds all the more ferocious and frightening. Yet Andrea slept solidly during her first two hours off. She fell asleep the moment her head touched the pillow. And she knew why. It was because Duncan was near. His presence was all she needed. She had forgotten what it was like to feel happy. Those

months when she had been besotted with Lucas
had not really been happy ones. They had been a
tortured existence when her hormones had been
stronger than her conscience and her sense of
right and wrong had abseiled out of the window.

She blamed Lucas for his empty promises and
cool lies; but she knew now that the blame lay
with herself too. Yet she also recognised clearly
the need to forgive herself, to close the door on
the past. Let herself off the hook. She had done
everything she could to end the affair when she'd
known he was married, his wife's face always in
mind.

Andrea was drifting back to consciousness in
her darkened cabin, almost lulled into a lullaby of
security, when a massive hundred-and-thirty-foot
wave smashed into the accommodation section.
She shot bolt upright as windows shattered, doors
splintered and electrical equipment sparked. A
clamour of voices rose above the howling wind
and pounding seas.

Major rig disaster. The phrase hammered her
brain with mega-sized blows as she pulled on her
outer clothes in the semi-darkness. Emergency
lighting came on with flooding relief. Her familiar
surroundings were in a crazy, disorientated state,
people running, voices raised. An egg-shell china
cup lay smashed on the floor.

Duncan appeared in the doorway, staggering
from wall to wall, out of breath. 'Are you all

right?' he gasped, pulling her up to him. His arms closed round her, shutting out the noise and the tumult. They kissed deeply with a plunging, breathless rapture. There was no time for anything more.

'I'm all right,' she whispered.

'Keep near me, darling.'

'Always,' she murmured, but drawing away from him all the same, inflamed by his embrace. She felt weak too near him.

'Bring your survival suit. We're not in danger of ditching but you never know.'

'And your injured driller? Is he being looked after?'

'He's stabilised. He's going to be all right.'

'This awful suit. . .'

'Have it by you.'

Sick-bay was crowded with walking wounded but had not itself been damaged. Many of the crew had been cut by flying glass; others had minor injuries. One man survived being hurled through an interior wall when the wave struck him as he lay in his bunk. He had broken ribs and possible concussion. The driller's pulse-rate was beginning to rise from the normal seventy-two for adults to a worrying hundred-plus. At the same time his temperature was slowly dropping.

'I don't like this at all,' said Duncan. 'I'll check him again. I must have missed something. There must be something I haven't noticed.'

He looked worried. It was every doctor's nightmare, missing something obvious. Yet every diagnosis was like solving a mystery; there were only so many clues.

'Internal bleeding is always concealed,' he was talking to himself now. 'One deduces it from the history of the injury, a rising pulse-rate and shock symptoms.'

'Perhaps he was also hit elsewhere but doesn't remember it now. The pipe could have rebounded.'

'That could be the answer. The pipe rebounded. I'll examine his chest and abdomen again. I wish we could get him off the rig. I want him in hospital. Has he coughed up any blood?'

'No.'

'The lungs may be OK, then.'

Some of the women catering staff had been cut by flying glass. Joan had face and jaw wounds. She was so shocked she could not speak, her eyes glazed with fear.

'Try not to worry,' said Andrea, searching the wounds for any shards of glass. 'There's no damage to your vocal cords. Your voice will come back soon. Shock can do funny things. It'll return to normal as your wounds heal. And your face will be fine. I always do very neat stitching but I'll take extra care because it's your face. There might be a bit of a scar on your forehead but a wispy fringe will cover that.'

The other woman had a deep wound in the palm of her hand. It was bleeding profusely. Andrea immediately pressed the point of the large artery to stop the bleeding.

'Now I want you to grasp this rolled-up bandage firmly. It'll help control the bleeding. There's no glass in your hand so I'll put on a sterile gauze dressing and a hand bandage, but it's really important to keep squeezing the rolled-up bandage.'

'And I thought you had an easy job, just doling out the odd aspirin and laxative,' the woman grimaced at the crowded surgery. It was like a battle-field. 'I'm sorry to have messed up your nice clean floor.'

'Nothing a drop of disinfectant won't mop up. It's more important that we make sure your pastry hand doesn't lose its light touch.'

Some of the crew appeared in survival suits. 'Waiting for the next big wave,' they said cheerfully.

'The rig is not in any danger,' said Andrea to her patients, trying to reassure them. But outside the teeth of the gale tore at the structure, howling through any open space.

The wind was up to a hundred and eighty knots. Another huge wave lashed the starboard side and tore away one of the two large lifeboats with a great splitting and violent wrenching of wood.

'There she goes,' said Duncan looking up

calmly. The boat sailed darkly past the window, narrowly missing part of the structure, turning turtle as the wave curled over and thrashed the flare tower.

'I think I'm beginning to feel sea-sick,' said Andrea, dry-mouthed, her forehead coming out in a cold sweat.

'Get some air if you can,' said Duncan. 'Take a nought point six milligram hyoscine hydrobromide tablet and sip some cold water. And don't drive.'

Andrea smiled limply. He was not as unsympathetic as he sounded, just very busy. Motion sickness could affect anyone, even the most experienced seafarers.

He touched her arm. 'Do as I say, take something for it, Andrea. I can't do without you here. This storm's not over yet.'

The recreation room was turned into another casualty area. The catering staff were producing relays of tea and coffee and soup. Anyone trained in first-aid was helping with cleaning cuts, strapping sprains, doling out reassurance. Tom Groves organised a roll call; one person was missing. The helicopter pilot.

'He's probably gone up to the helideck to make sure his precious machine is securely tethered. Damned fool. Everyone was told to stay inside.'

Andrea handed Duncan a mug of coffee. There was a slight lull. They had a twenty-second breath-

ing space. Andrea leaned wearily against the edge
of the couch, anything to take the weight off her
feet.

'Did you mean what you said. . .earlier,' she
asked.

'What did I say?' He was dragging it out of her.

'You called me darling.'

He moved over to stand beside her. It seemed
that there was only the two of them in that
crowded space. They carved a shell of silence
around them. He blinked down at her, a smile
hovering on his mouth.

'Well, so I did now, and I never say anything I
don't mean,' he said in a low voice.

'But you told me. . .a while back. . .that you
had met someone special. . .'

'For an intelligent woman, you can be pretty
dumb at times. Yes, I have met someone special,
someone very special.'

'Then. . . ?'

'When the storm is over and all my patients are
safely in hospital, I shall take time, a lot of time,
telling you just how special that woman is. And
by the time I've finished telling you, I think you'll
know who she is.'

He finished his coffee in a gulp. 'Now back to
work, Sister, and no slacking.'

There was another moment during the storm
when Andrea had a space to herself. She ran to

her cabin and rummaged in a drawer for a small box, and in it was a man's ring, a flamboyant signet ring.

Andrea struggled back on deck, trying to find a safe place that was near the sea, but not too near. Spray dashed up black and silvery, plumes of water veiling the turmoil below. She threw the ring into the waves with all her might.

'No, I don't want your ring, Lucas,' she shouted. 'I'm letting myself off the hook. I'm not carrying around your guilt any longer.'

She let her hatred go, forgiving herself for hating him. Closing the wound, closing the past, accepting the scar that she wore close to her heart, unable now to believe that she had kept the ring for so long.

Pete Overton appeared out of a fog of water. 'What on earth are you doing out here, Sister? It isn't safe.'

'Just letting go of the past.'

'Not sensible in this weather. I'll take you back.'

'Tell me, Pete. Why do you avoid me? I've noticed it, time and time again.'

He grinned, his face drenched. 'You're far too pretty, Sister. And I'm engaged to a nice girl back home. I thought I'd better keep out of temptation's way.'

Andrea hung on to his arm for support. 'I'm so relieved. I thought it was some deep-seated problem or perhaps something that I'd said. When we're back to normal, you must tell me about your fiancée over coffee and a doughnut.'

'I think that's a date,' he said in a friendly way.

CHAPTER TEN

THE battering of Lochinvar went on for seven hours into the early hours of the morning. All the mighty elements joined forces against these pesky midgets who dared to live balanced on a precarious structure over the water. The city on the sea was completely cut off from the world. Radio communications failed. Production was shut down. Makeshift repairs were made on the wrecked area of accommodation to keep out the rain and wind and prevent further damage from high seas.

Only when the casualties were reduced to a trickle could Andrea close her eyes for a few moments. She had no idea of the time. It had stood still somewhere in the middle of the pounding waves and howling wind. Clumsy crystal drops still spattered the windows.

She sat on the edge of a cabinet with her chin in her hands. She felt tired and lonely and suddenly lacking in hope, worn out by inner emptiness. Had she dreamed those few sweet words in her cabin? Her heart steeled itself not to imagine more. Duncan had not by so much of a flicker of his eyelids referred to them again. She wanted to sleep, not just for a few hours but for several weeks.

He was bending over a burly roughneck who had a handful of deck splinters, being as gentle as if he was treating a trembling five-year-old school-boy. He became aware of her candid eyes on him, saw the quiver touching the corners of her full mouth.

'Pack it in,' said Duncan, coming over when he had taken out the last splinter, drying his hands for the hundredth time. 'I can see to everyone now.'

He wrapped her in a flinty, humorous smile that she imagined told her a thousand words. She wanted to reach out to him, to feel the rough friction of his skin against her own silky smooth-ness. Instead she shook her head, her hair coming loose from its clip.

'We can't stop. There's too much to do. I've got to clear up and put things straight for tomorrow; there are the two patients who need constant care. There's still a lot going for a working partnership.' Even if nothing else ever works, she wanted to add.

'I've been saying that for weeks, Sister. If you worked ashore at my hospital, it could be a real working partnership every day,' said Duncan. 'Of course, we couldn't pay you as much as on a rig.'

'Not that old song again. You never give up, do

you? Do I have to remind you about my father's debts? They haven't gone away.'

'I want you safely ashore. Haven't I made myself clear yet? Surely tonight has been enough,' he glowered. 'I don't want you out here. Rig work is not suitable for a woman and this storm tonight proves my point a hundredfold.'

'The storm doesn't prove anything,' said Andrea, standing up straight, brushing down her clothes, then flinging instruments into the sterilizer. 'A male medic would not have worked any faster or coped more efficiently than I am. If you're talking about physical stamina, then OK, I can't lift heavy patients but there are always enough roughnecks around to help. But as for longterm stamina, I'll still be going strong when many a muscle-bound male would be flaked out, snoring his head off on a bunk.'

Duncan gave a deep sigh, his face unreadable, even his energy at a low level. 'You are making it so difficult for me, lass. Can't you read between the lines? I'm not good at this. I've been trying to tell you that you are a wonderful nurse, one of the best, and I've given up trying to cancel your contract, but I can't bear to spend every day worrying whether you've fallen off the rig or been hit by a swinging crane.'

There was a shocked pause. Andrea wondered if she had heard correctly, or if her tired mind was imagining the care and concern in his voice.

'I'm glad that at last you've admitted I can do the job and I'm touched that you're concerned about my safety.' Tears glistened on Andrea's lashes and she turned away so that he could not see. The moment told her the secret in her heart. It came with such a stab of pain that for a moment her happiness was tossed aside. She loved him. She wanted him. But this was a different love. She wanted nothing for herself, only for him. Everything for him.

'When the storm is over and we get back on-shore, we must spend some time together. A lot of time; in fact I want to spend all my time with you.' Duncan leaned across and brushed some of the tangled hair from her face. 'There's a foot-path, a bit rocky in places, through Glen Esk from Gannachy Bridge alongside the ravine of the river. It's quite beautiful. You'd like it and I want to show you. Queen Victoria used to take pony rides along there.'

There it was again. His pride in Aberdeen and the Scottish countryside. But now he wanted to share it with her. She did not know where to look. The air was seeded with moisture, hung on the rim of a growing intensity between them, waiting with unspoken thoughts.

'Or we could go and see my Uncle Angus, take a walk round the distillery, pretend we're tourists. He'd like to meet you.'

She had to laugh and it was a soft happy sound. 'Gosh, a choice. Queen Victoria or Uncle Angus.'

She felt a wistful longing to walk at his side through some rugged glen, to take his hand, to talk about everything under the sun. This was just what she wanted, what she needed to heal the hurt, an uncomplicated companionship, out in the open. How could she ever have thought that meeting Lucas on the sly was happiness? She must have been mad.

'I think I'd like to walk,' said Andrea. 'I've got new walking boots and they need walking in with something gentle. A trek to the head of the glen sounds ideal.' Then she remembered all the other things he was proud of, his family, wanted to share in his pride. 'But I'd also like to see round the distillery, a wee tasting.'

She was laughing at him now but he did not mind.

'Come outside.' His voice was measured and precise and serious. He took her arm and propelled her out into the corridor. 'I want to talk to you.'

'Is it safe?' She meant the storm outside.

'No, it isn't,' he said almost roughly, meaning his sudden urgency. 'But I want a little privacy and for once you'll listen to me without interrupting.'

The corridor was half open to the elements. A sheet of tarpaulin had been hastily nailed over a broken window and it billowed and flapped like a khaki sail. The sounds of the storm burst onto their eardrums, the howling banshee wind, the roaring, thunderous waves.

Andrea drifted towards the gaping hole. She was disorientated, had lost all sense of direction and now it was obvious she did not know where she was going. She leaned back, blinking against the stinging rain, against the ragged, beating wings of wind tearing at her clothes. The lightning sky was a vast disorder of flying shapes and racing clouds.

'I'm scared,' said Andrea, without thinking, shivering, reacting immediately to his tall, reassuring presence striding to her side. She could not resist the urge to run to him, to burrow into his arms.

'That's better, that's exactly what I want to hear,' said Duncan, pulling her roughly into the shelter of his arms. 'Come here and listen to me, once and for all, you stubborn woman. I'm only gong to tell you one time.'

'I'm not going. You can't make me. I'm not leaving,' she cried, her voice full of anguish, her hair becoming plastered in dark glossy streaks across her forehead. 'I have to work on the rig. I've told you before, my father died and left a lot of debts. He had cancer but didn't tell anyone. Didn't even tell me, kept it all to himself. My salary from the rig goes to the repayments on the house. I've pledged the whole year's salary. If I don't pay them off, my mother will lose her house. I can't let that happen. Her home means everything to her. She couldn't move. She's lived there all her married life.'

Duncan gripped her arms with a fierce joy. He saw the tears mingling with rain on her face.

'Will you stop talking now? I'm glad it's never been a selfish financial motive for your ridiculous determination to work the rigs. I approve of the concern you feel for your mother and your determination. But surely there are other ways of solving that problem? Isn't there an insurance mortgage that would let your mother live on in her house but where the insurance company takes the house when your mother eventually dies.'

'You don't understand,' Andrea wailed, shaking her head. 'It's already mortgaged to the hilt. They'll foreclose if I don't continue to pay it off. What'll happen? What else can I do? I'm not a financial wizard.' She was torturing herself with empty questions.

'I think you should start sharing some of your problems instead of trying to solve everything yourself. No wonder you can't sleep. Your head is buzzing with thoughts, robbing you of that much needed rest and relaxation. No wonder your. . . eyes. . .look tired.'

Duncan had been going to say 'lovely eyes' but the words stuck in his throat. Would she know that was what he meant? Whenever was he going to say what he really felt for her? For the first time in his life, everything was clear, yet he couldn't tell her. He cursed his puritan upbringing, where people didn't say what they meant. Where people didn't speak of love, hug or kiss their children.

'I'll use a cold compress,' said Andrea.

'When you didn't see me for a while, I went to Skye where I could have a peaceful couple of days, walking the moors and sailing. The Cuillin Hills are great for rock-climbing. And for thinking. Andrea, I did a lot of thinking.'

'Thinking about us, about me. . .?' Andrea clutched at the hope.

'When are you going to start believing me? I've been trying to tell you for weeks.'

'Tell me what? You've certainly got a funny way of trying to tell me something,' said Andrea, near to tears. 'Biting my head off at every opportunity.'

'They were all love bites,' said Duncan uncompromisingly, kissing her throat, her neck, her ears. His hands were pressing her close, and she could feel the heat despite the rain and the wind.

They were both getting soaked but it did not seem to matter. His shoulders were becoming dark patches. She knew her shirt was already clinging and revealing the curve of her breasts but she did not care. Duncan locked his arms under

her armpits and was lifting her against him. She
felt the long line of his thighs and hipbones
trapping her body. His dark eyes were full of
sultry passion that shocked her southern coolness.
But as his mouth took possession of her lips, she
felt the same explosion of feeling taking hold
of her. She made no effort to hold back her
response. It was impossible.

'I love you, love you, love,' she murmured but
she did not know if he heard.

This would be no cautious, gentle courtship. It
was a frenzy of loving that rocked them to the
core, wild and seeking. They treasured every
sense, the smell, the touch, the feel of each other.
The voice of her body took her on a rushing,
hastening journey that radiated with joy.

'Andrea?' he asked, taking in air from their
kissing. 'Doesn't this tell you something? Do I
have to spell it all out? I love you. You're the
special woman I said I had met. My very special
woman. The woman I want in my life. I don't
want anyone else. I love you.'

'You love me. . .?'

'I've been falling in love with you and running
scared. I made a mistake once, oh, years ago, and
I didn't ever want to make another. But now I'm
sure. I can't live without you. Andrea, what do
you say? Will you marry me?'

She was hearing everything she had ever wanted
to hear. Slowly she savoured the look of him so

that she would remember the moment for ever. The rain-streaked face, the wet hair, his eyes deep with love.

'Yes,' she said. 'I will.'

His eyes softened, glowed. 'I can't wait for you. I want to make love to you. Oh, my darling, I won't be so clumsy again.'

'Duncan, it wasn't you. It was me. I was caught in a trap, remembering something from the past that was all over, long ago but still hurt. A terrible mistake that I made and have paid for over and over again. If only I could turn back the clock, it would never have happened. . .'

He put his finger gently against the torrent of words.

'No more, my darling. The past is over and done with. Now it's just you and me together.

Andrea's mouth softened with longing. This time she would not resist him. All that foolishness and hurt had gone, long buried in the past. 'We will. . .we will. I love you. I want you so much. When the storm's over and our patients are all right. . .'

'Hell, Andrea,' he said, pulling her close. 'Why couldn't I have fallen in love with someone who doesn't put other people first? Somebody ordinary and normal who would put us first.'

They stood in rapture and surprise at the new-ness of their love with their two figures wrapped as if one, shoulders to thighs, her breasts aching against him, their longing burning through their wet clothes.

'Could you make Hunter's Lodge our home?' he asked, gravelly, hesitant, as if afraid she might want a new house, smart and modern, somewhere on the outskirts of Aberdeen.

'I love your house. I want to live there with you, grow roses in the conservatory, keep your sister's room at the ready,' said Andrea, her eyes luminous and tender. 'Iron your shirts properly.'

'And there's the coachhouse flat. . .do you think your mother could ever bring herself to leave Hastings and come and live in the coach-house? It would help her financial problems and she would still have her independence. Supposing at first she came for the summer season and let her house at Hastings? That would bring in an income, wouldn't it?'

'Oh, Duncan, what a marvellous idea. We could ask her to come for a holiday and see how she likes it. She might fall in love with Aberdeen. It's such a fascinating city and all those flowers. . . she'd love the flowers and the rivers and the sea. She's always lived by the sea.'

He touched a swirl of her hair. 'And what about us? We deserve a holiday too.'

'I've never been to the Isle of Skye,' she suggested, their tanned fingers laced.

'Never been to the Isle of Skye? My darling Andrea, you haven't lived. It is the most beautiful island in the Highlands, with a coastline that seems to stretch for a thousand miles. The sea is magnificent and the views breathtaking. We could sail, and walk and climb and in the evening eat locally caught lobster or crab.'

'We needn't do much thinking,' she teased.

The proud Scot held her face and looked deeply into her smoky eyes, ran his thumb gently along her dark brows. 'Not that kind of thinking. Come with me Andrea. Let's make it very special, a honeymoon. Just you and me, away from everyone. Don't let's waste any more time. Come to Skye with me. We'll walk in your new boots. . .' He kissed her deeply, hungrily, a soft and slow embrace that was full of promise. 'I want you with me so much. It would be wonderful for a honeymoon, away from everyone, everything.'

Andrea felt peace invading her mind and her body. There was a strength in his rugged, handsome face that made her heart quicken. He was right. They were meant for each other. She wanted to feel the heat of his body against her own. She wanted to share that secret voyaging. She wanted to lie warmly entwined while the wild weather raged outside. Her womanhood was a silken core that longed for his love.

'I may not be able to wait till then,' she said, feeling his hard chest, knowing she was ripe for love. She had never spoken to any man like this.

But this time it was right to be honest, to say what she meant.

'But not Morag's room.'

'In case she comes in to wash her hair.'

'The storm is nearly over,' he said tenderly as she lifted her mouth to him, her lips parting.

'My poor birds,' she murmured. 'They'll be so hungry.'

'Then let's go and feed the poor things,' he said. 'You and I, together. In a moment.'

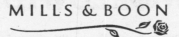

Barbara

DELINSKY

A COLLECTION

New York Times bestselling author Barbara Delinsky has created three wonderful love stories featuring the charming and irrepressible matchmaker, Victoria Lesser. Worldwide are proud to bring back these delightful romances — together for the first time, they are published in one beautiful volume this September.

THE REAL THING
TWELVE ACROSS
A SINGLE ROSE

Available from September   **Priced £4.99**

W❂RLDWIDE

NORA ROBERTS

◆

SWEET REVENGE

Adrianne's glittering lifestyle was the perfect foil for her extraordinary talents — no one knew her as *The Shadow*, the most notorious jewel thief of the decade. She had a secret ambition to carry out the ultimate heist — one that would even an old and bitter score. But she would need all her stealth and cunning to pull it off, with Philip Chamberlain, Interpol's toughest and smartest cop, hot on her trail. His only mistake was to fall under Adrianne's seductive spell.

AVAILABLE NOW   **PRICE £4.99**

WORLDWIDE

Available from WH Smith, John Menzies, Volume One, Forbuoys, Martins, Woolworths, Tesco, Asda, Safeway and other paperback stockists.

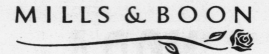

MILLS & BOON